The Par ꙫ

Th_ _ _ne
Algarve _rime Thrillers
written by

Trevor Holman

To Pauling
Best Wishes

For my very good friend
the real Mrs Gemma Borgert

Copyright © Trevor Holman (2020)

Trevor Holman can be contacted by email at:

info@trevorholman.net

Principal Characters appearing in the book

The Algarve, Southern Portugal
Michael Turner
Me, a murder mystery & travel writer
Dr Samantha Turner
My wife, a private doctor based in Quinta do Lago

Paris, France
Mrs Gemma Louise Borgert / Lady Louise
Hamilton Smythe
The Paris Poisoner
Oscar Dubois
Editor of Le Figaro Newspaper
Pierre Faucheux
News Editor at Le Figaro
Detective Chief Inspector Claude Moreau
Police Nationale, formerly known as the Sûreté
Detective Inspector Hugo Duchand
Police Nationale

Dr Gaspard Boucher
Doctor in Paris
Raphael D'Aurevilly
Executive Chef at Restaurant 'Seulement le meilleur'
Baron Francois Leblanc
Owner of Restaurant 'Seulement le meilleur'

Amsterdam, Netherlands
Chief Superintendent Helena Van Houten
Interpol Officer - Head of European Operations
Martin Smith
Interpol Officer - Covert Operative & Specialist Burglar
Inspector George Copeland
Interpol Officer - Senior Pilot & Covert Operative
Inspector Colin O'Donnell
Interpol Officer - Co Pilot & Covert Operative
Sergeant Jo Sylvester
Interpol Officer - Covert Operative

England, United Kingdom
Lord Charles Hamilton Smythe
Lady Louise's father
Lady Emily Hamilton Smythe
Lady Louise's mother

Preface

Charlie Smith started his working life at the age of 12 working most evenings and weekends on his father's hardware and knick-knack stall on Beresford Square Market in Woolwich, South London, where he was born and grew up. Charlie didn't have a middle name, he was just 'Charlie'. He asked his dad once why he wasn't like most of the other boys at his school who did have a middle name. Charlie's dad joked and told him they simply couldn't afford a middle name as well. Charlie thought he was serious and meant it, so he just let it go. Charlie was what most people would describe as coming from a working class background, but he was also really bright, even as a kid, and his dad soon recognized that Charlie was absolutely brilliant at spotting opportunities. Over the years he chatted up various friends of his dad, relations, school mates, in fact anyone he met who he thought could be useful to him. Having 'the gift of the gab' as his dad called it, Charlie persuaded them to make his little inventions and ideas, nothing grand, just small practical things. Five years later Charlie had created his own little empire of small workshops in various sheds and garages in the area where he'd now got all sorts of people making him bits and bobs, this and that, and all as cheaply as possible. Charlie then sold the workshops output for decent profits on the market. After another couple of years and with a decent amount of cash in the bank, Charlie decided if he was going to do really well in life then he needed to acquire some serious 'proper' knowledge. So Charlie enrolled at a local night school where he studied religiously, and at the end of three years of hard work Charlie received a diploma in advanced electrical engineering. By the time he was 23 Charlie had negotiated with the help of his bank manager a very nice deal to buy his first small factory in Greenwich, South London.

By way of celebration, and while he was waiting for all the legalities and paperwork to be approved and finalized, Charlie decided he would treat himself to a three week holiday, eventually deciding on something quiet and relaxing, a leisurely walking, rambling and sightseeing holiday basing himself in a nice hotel in the town of Hamilton in South Lanarkshire. Hamilton is located in the central Lowlands of Scotland, roughly ten miles south-east of Glasgow and about 35 miles south-west of Edinburgh, and that holiday changed Charlie's life.

While he was out walking one day he met and got chatting to a very pretty young girl from Edinburgh named Emily Bunce. She was also on holiday in the area and as far as Charlie was concerned, Emily was without doubt the most beautiful woman he had ever seen, and Charlie being Charlie and doing nothing by halves, he fell instantly in love with her. Emily was ambitious too, but her main aim in life had always been to marry someone, preferably rich, who could keep her in the manner to which she was yet to become accustomed, but most important of all, it would mean she could get rid of what she considered to be her absolutely dreadful surname of Bunce. Extremely pretty though she was, and love her as much as he did, Charlie had no illusions about Emily, and he recognized straight away that Emily was at heart an out and out snob, and when she eventually discovered Charlie's surname was Smith she was utterly appalled. It was so dreadfully common.

However, they'd both fallen in love with each other, and when towards the end of the second week Charlie asked her to marry him, she said yes, but only on one strict condition. She insisted Charlie must change his name immediately by deed poll. Emily had obviously been thinking about it as she had it all planned. Charlie Smith would become Charles Hamilton Smythe. 'Charles' she said was very aristocratic whereas 'Charlie' was just plain common, 'Hamilton' in honour of and a permanent reminder of where they had met and fallen in love, and 'Smythe' as an acceptable alternative to Smith. Charlie laughed at the idea, but he could see she was serious and it was the only way of getting the woman he loved down the aisle, so what the heck! Charlie agreed and the following day they went together to the Town Hall where he legally changed his name. During the third week of Charlie's holiday they decided there was no point in waiting to be married. Emily had no great prospects in Scotland and nothing keeping her there, so at Charlie's suggestion they stopped off at a small wedding chapel in Gretna Green on the way back to London where they got married becoming Mr Charles and Mrs Emily Hamilton Smythe. Soon after they were married, Emily told everyone she met, including all of Charlie's workers that from now on her husband must always be addressed as Mr Charles, and never Charlie, and wanting a quiet life with the woman he loved, he reluctantly agreed. With her husband's initiatives, brilliant ideas and non-stop work ethic, plus his fast growing reputation in the industrial world, success came upon success, and over the following years that success brought with it vast amounts of wealth, which enabled Charlie and Emily to buy what she'd always dreamed of, a large Palladian style country mansion and estate on the outskirts of Berkshire. But for Emily by far the most important aspect to Mrs Hamilton Smythe, was success came with honours. Firstly, her husband received a knighthood in the New Year's Honours list and then six years later Charlie was made a peer, becoming Lord Hamilton Smythe. Needless to say Charlie's wife was mildly ecstatic about introducing herself to everyone she met as the very aristocratic sounding Lady Emily Hamilton Smythe.

Their marriage had actually gone extremely well, and a few years after they had been married Emily had brought a daughter into the world, but sadly after she had given birth Emily was informed by the doctors at the hospital that she could sadly have no more children. They'd named their daughter Gemma Louise, and as she grew up you could both see and tell that thankfully she'd inherited her mother's good looks and her father's sharp intellect and demeanour, and luckily not the other way round. Knowing the child would be their only offspring, Emily had devoted her life to her daughter from the moment she'd been born, and consequently she had spoilt her rotten. Charlie had chosen the name Gemma in honour of his late aunt and Godmother, but Emily didn't think Gemma was anywhere near aristocratic enough, so on her mother's insistence her daughter was always known by the name Emily had chosen for her, and from the age of one her young daughter was always addressed as Lady Louise Hamilton Smythe.

Again, Charlie let it pass, but to him she would always be his beautiful Gemma.

Growing up Lady Louise had wanted for nothing. Thanks to her father's wealth she had received a brilliant education attending Cheltenham Ladies College and then on to Oxford where she had studied and obtained her degree in medicine. However, with Lady Louise having graduated, her mother eventually persuaded her that 'proper and cultured young ladies' like herself did not 'work' and associate with the lower classes, but instead they mingled at select dinner parties and balls with the right sort of people, enjoyed life and found themselves a suitable husband.

Lady Louise had always had a host of male admirers, but none had ever really appealed to her, until one evening where she attended a gala ball at her old college in Oxford. As well as previous graduates from the college, invites had also been sent out to a few select medical graduates who had all distinguished themselves in one way or another at some of Europe's top universities. Among those who received an invite, happily accepted it and attended the ball was a handsome young surgeon from Germany named Matthias Borgert. Lady Louise was also like her mother in one other respect, and that was that when she fell in love it was instant and it was all consuming. Lady Louise Hamilton Smythe much to her own surprise discovered she was totally and utterly in love for the first time in her life, and fortunately for her the young Matthias felt exactly the same.

Unfortunately for them both however, Lady Emily despised anyone who did not have an upper class English upbringing, which was rich coming from a woman who was born into a working class Scottish family named Bunce. However, Lady Louise realized that without a shadow of doubt her mother would object to any marriage for her beloved daughter outside of the English upper classes. Lady Louise also knew that her mother would undoubtedly interfere and create as many problems as she could for them both, so they vowed to keep their relationship a total secret, and then when the time was right they would also get married in secret. They succeeded with their secrecy, and just two short months after they first met, Lady Louise, choosing to use her other Christian name of Gemma to avoid detection by her mother, married the man she loved and Lady Louise Hamilton Smythe became Mrs Gemma Louise Borgert in a small chapel in an equally small village in the heart of rural Worcestershire. The only people that knew of the marriage were the happy couple themselves, the quite elderly vicar who had married them and was on the verge of retirement, and the two passing strangers who had acted as their witnesses.

The following day, Gemma and Matthias flew to Paris for a very discreet week long honeymoon, booking into a middle of the road three star hotel as the newly married Mr and Mrs Humphries. They had explained to the receptionist that they had only been married ten hours, only just arrived in Paris, and it being the weekend and with everywhere closed until Monday, they obviously hadn't had a chance to get passports or ID organised in their married name of Humphries, although they had an appointment to sort everything when the Consulate office opened on Monday. The receptionist, a young girl in her early twenties readily accepted their story, took pity on them as newlyweds and said they could stay over the weekend, but must produce either passports or ID cards by Monday night, once the British Consulate was open. On their first night they never left the hotel, but on their second night, Matthias insisted on taking his new wife to a very upmarket Parisian restaurant for an exquisite meal. They both loved good food, and they both loved good wine, and they both had a wonderful time, but shortly after returning to their hotel room Matthias started complaining of quite severe stomach pains. Gemma rang the reception desk and having been put through to a help line she summoned urgent medical help straight away, but as it turned out the doctor they'd called was busy with another patient and he only appeared at their hotel door an hour and twenty minutes later, by which time Matthias was doubled up on the bed and screaming in absolute agony. The doctor, who had heard the screams through the door entered their hotel room, and just as he crossed the threshold Matthias stopped screaming. He had died. The doctor rushed over to the bed but it was too late, and all he could do was pronounce Gemma's new husband dead. The doctor signed the death certificate stating it was 'accidental food poisoning', and then he repeated the same to the police officer that attended the scene. The gendarme was very sympathetic, but he was also quick to point out that as this was an 'accidental' death, no prosecutions would follow, although they would obviously be having a strong word with the restaurant. The doctor made a telephone call and arranged for a local funeral company to collect the deceased and an hour later, the doctor, the gendarme and Matthias Humphries all left the hotel.

Completely distraught and alone in her bed that night, Gemma Borgert reflected on all that had happened. She acknowledged to herself that she was obviously in a very emotional state, but nevertheless it stood to reason that her husband had been killed, and despite the so called 'accidental' label, in her opinion those responsible needed punishing, and she quickly came to the conclusion that if the French authorities weren't going to punish anyone, she would have to punish the guilty parties herself. The question she had to ask herself however was; who exactly was to blame?

In her thoughts she went through all that had happened once more and who in her opinion was responsible. She obviously blamed the chef for preparing, cooking and serving poisonous food, and she blamed the restaurant for allowing him to do so. She blamed the Paris police who had made it perfectly clear that they were not going to prosecute one of Paris's top chefs or their precious upmarket Parisian restaurant for a so called 'accident'. Gemma also blamed the doctor and along with him the Parisian health service in general for being totally useless and completely uncaring in not acting quickly enough, and therefore not rushing to save her husband's life. Eventually, and after much thought and careful deliberation, Mrs Gemma Borgert came to the clear conclusion that having reasoned it through, her husband's death was in reality the fault of all Parisians because of their totally selfish attitude to life, as in her opinion, the people of Paris, like most of the French nation, are all far too full of themselves and couldn't care less about anybody else.

That night Mrs Borgert set about planning her revenge on the people of Paris. With her Oxford degree in medicine she certainly had the medical knowledge she would need, and thanks to her loving father she also had the money to pay for whatever she needed. But best of all by far, she suddenly realized that nobody in the whole world apart from three doddery old age pensioners in a remote Worcestershire parish church knew who Mrs Borgert was. As for Paris, well the hotel receptionist, the doctor and the police only knew them as Mr and Mrs Humphries.

Gemma Borgert decided she would from that moment on take on two totally separate and completely different personas in order to achieve her objective of total revenge. Firstly, that of the delightfully polite, extremely elegant and genteel Lady Louise Hamilton Smythe, and secondly, the revengeful Mrs Gemma Borgert who was going to punish Paris in every way she could for killing her husband and totally destroying her life. She realised that she needed to remain anonymous, so Gemma packed all her and Matthias's clothes and belongings into their two suitcases, and at 3.00 am, unseen by anyone and without paying, she left the hotel via a rear door. Gemma flew back to the UK where she spent two weeks preparing everything she would need for the coming few weeks, and having completed everything, she then flew back to Paris, ready to begin taking her revenge.

Chapter One

Hi, my name is Michael Turner, and over the previous few years I had become a reasonably successful author, originally writing what turned out to be incredibly lucrative murder mysteries, of which twelve had now been published worldwide. However, lucrative as they were, I decided I both wanted and needed a change. I started writing travel guide books, but homing in on real crime locations for the traveller to visit that wants to do more than just lay on a beach slowly roasting in the sun, and for added interest I also include locations that have been used in films and TV series based around crime. They seem to be selling quite well, and having recently finished my fifth and by far the biggest guide, Spain, I'm now working on my sixth travel guide.

My wife lovely wife Sam, who despite regular protests is still called Samantha by her parents, was a very successful doctor in the UK, and an occasional police surgeon, working mainly with the Metropolitan police in South London, but she then moved to Portugal where she now runs her own private medical practice. It's located in an area of the Algarve in southern Portugal known as Quinta do Lago, which is where we met and where we live. To be honest, there are some days when I wish that was all we did, me writing books and Sam seeing her patients. But then a few years ago everything changed for us when Malcolm Tisbury, one of my neighbours was brutally murdered in his own home. To cut a long story short, Sam and I somehow got involved in trying to find the killer. We worked with both the local police, who are known as the GNR, the London, or the more correctly entitled Metropolitan police, and then finally Interpol. Somehow or other we ended up going undercover, travelling to South Africa, the Bahamas and half of Europe in the process, but if I say so myself we did a pretty good job of bringing the man christened by the press as the Mijas Murderer to justice.

A few months later, we were approached again by the Metropolitan police and Interpol, and we were asked if we would help them in their search for a brilliant counterfeiter known only as the Faro Forger. We agreed to help if we could, but in the process we found we had somehow agreed to be 'part time' Interpol officers, helping out when asked. They even gave us badges and warrant cards and suddenly our amateur detective work had become official. Despite our thinking the Faro Forger would be a simple local case, yet again our undercover investigations took us all over the world, and having successfully found the Faro Forger and concluded the investigation we thought life would get back to normal. It did - for all of sixteen days. The first fourteen of those days Sam and I spent on our honeymoon, and we'd only been back just over twenty four hours when Sam received a phone call from the Salzburg police informing her that her ex flat mate had committed suicide, and Sam's name was still listed in her friends passport as the point of contact in an emergency. Knowing her as well as she did, Sam refused to believe her friend would have taken her own life, and so we were off again looking into what became known as the Salzburg Suicides. Sam's friend had been just one of several murders made to look like suicides, but thankfully that case was eventually concluded with both of us surprisingly still in one piece, and for a couple of months life calmed down. Then most unexpectedly we were approached by the head of operations at MI5, a guy named Craig Overton, who having met us briefly during the Salzburg Suicides investigations, asked us if we would be prepared to go undercover for him and the UK government, this time in Egypt, as the terrorists MI5 were interested in would recognize all of his own MI5 undercover agents, and they'd also know both the CIA and Mossad agents, so he couldn't ask for their help. I have to say, when your own Prime Minister asks you personally to do something for your country it is extremely difficult to refuse. I won't bother to go into all the details, but the Cairo Conspiracy as Craig ended up calling it only ended fairly recently, and I'm very pleased to say that I'm now spending my mornings writing my travel books and Sam spends her mornings doctoring.

Thankfully money is not a problem for us. We're not rich, but I think we are what most people would describe as comfortably off, and bearing that in mind we both made the decision to take afternoons and weekends off, and we spend plenty of time relaxing, visiting friends and basically doing what we want. Very recently Sam and I reluctantly got talked into trying our hand at golf by a good friend and his wife who live locally to us, and despite our initial wariness we are actually quite enjoying it. Neither of us is very good yet, but we're taking lessons, we enjoy the exercise and most importantly we love the opportunity to sit and chat with folk at the nineteenth tee, the golfers' term for the bar in the clubhouse. I have to say, I'm beginning to see the attraction, and I can also see why there are currently thirty eight golf courses in the Algarve, and no doubt even more will soon be built.

It was mine and Sam's second wedding anniversary, and I'd decided to take Sam to Paris for a long weekend to celebrate having spent two years of married bliss. Sam on the other hand described it as two years of total chaos, running round the world chasing murderers, forgers, master criminals, spies and terrorists, interspersed with a few brief moments of married bliss. Fortunately Sam did add a caveat in that she said she wouldn't have changed a minute of the last four years since we first met in Quinta do Lago in the Algarve, where we still live to this day. To be honest, I really love Portugal and couldn't imagine living anywhere else now.

We flew to Paris's Charles De Gaulle airport from Faro airport arriving around noon on the Friday, as later that evening I'd bought tickets for the new Cirque du Soleil performance at the Accor Hotels Arena. We watched our first Cirque du Soleil show called simply 'KA' at the MGM Grand in Las Vegas in 2017, and from that moment on we've loved every show they've ever put on. This one was no exception.

'So what do you want to do tomorrow?' I asked Sam.

'Oh, I don't know. How about a leisurely river boat cruise down the Seine, followed by a trip to the top of the Eiffel Tower and then in the evening a nice meal in a posh restaurant?' she relied.

'Anyone would imagine you'd been thinking about this in advance.' I smiled.

'Might have' she replied giggling.

'OK, we'll do a trip on the Seine and then have lunch at the top of the Eiffel Tower, but the restaurant we go to tomorrow evening has to provide a decent plain grilled steak and chips as well as all that really fancy stuff you like.'

'I really did marry a Philistine didn't I' Sam said.

'Oh Mrs Turner, it's far too late to change your mind now' I replied.

'Wouldn't want to' she said laughing and we headed back to the hotel.

On Saturday morning we took a river cruise on the Seine, and very pleasant it was. The sun was shining and sitting on the top deck with a couple of cool beers in our hands we watched Paris's many architectural wonders drift by. We gently cruised past the Eiffel Tower on our right, the gardens of the Trocadéro on our left, the Louvre also on our left, and after sailing under numerous bridges we approached the small island on which sits the magnificent Cathedral of Notre Dame. Having passed Notre Dame on our left, our cruise boat then turned left, went round the back of the island and returned us to our boarding point, the foot of the Eiffel Tower. As promised, we had a light lunch at the restaurant halfway up the tower and then we took the lift to the top for some amazing views of Paris. Around 7.30 pm, and dressed in our smartest clothes we headed off to the posh restaurant Sam had selected, and I have to say after our twenty minute walk to get there I was ready for my steak and chips. I know I'm a disappointment to my wife with my penchant for plain and simple English cooking, but as far as I'm concerned you can't beat steak and chips, steak and kidney pie, roast beef and Yorkshire pudding with a dozen roast potatoes or another of my all-time favourites, good old crumbed Wiltshire ham, two fried eggs and crinkly chips, preferably with two or three slices of white bread and butter and served in an English pub with a pint of lager. But that's me, a true philistine to the core. Sam despairs of me, but I blame my mother. Being an only child she spoilt me rotten and my limited list of food likes was the end result.

We'd been in the restaurant about an hour and we'd both really enjoyed the food. Sam had her fancy French cuisine, and I had enjoyed a really good sirloin steak and chips. The extremely helpful waiter even agreed to get me some onion rings even though they weren't on the menu. We had just ordered our desserts, when the man on the table next to us made a sort of croaking noise and then suddenly keeled over, falling onto the table and then slipping off his chair he fell onto the floor. His wife was screaming and everyone in the restaurant started panicking. Being a practising doctor, Sam's medical ethics kicked in immediately, and she quickly got down on her knees and examined the man. Thirty seconds or so after he'd landed on the floor Sam looked up at the man's wife;

'I'm so very sorry' she said 'I'm afraid your husband is dead'.

Before the poor man's wife could react to the dreadful news she'd just been told, another of the restaurant's customers, this time a woman sitting at a table for four the other side of the restaurant started clutching her throat and saying she couldn't breathe. She died in her chair a minute later. The police and an ambulance were called immediately, but despite their presence, during the following twenty minutes a further five of the restaurants patrons died, making a total of seven deaths in thirty minutes. For obvious reasons none of us were allowed to leave the restaurant, but the French Police allowed Sam and myself to talk to customers when we showed them our Interpol badges and IDs. We weren't officially working and we shouldn't really have got involved, but whoever had done this, and Sam and I both agreed it had to be deliberate poisoning by someone, they had nevertheless screwed up our wedding anniversary meal and I was to put it bluntly damned annoyed.

'Are you OK' Sam asked me.

'Yeah, I'm fine' I replied. 'Whatever it was they were given, thank God neither of us ate the food that contained the poison? I'm going to have a quick look at the dinner and dessert plates of all the people that have died and see if I can find a common denominator.'

I just wandered from table to table, trying not to look too inquisitive, and as far as I could see, the only food common to all the plates were tomatoes. Not cooked, just plain ordinary raw tomatoes. The plate of the man next to us had been cleared away, but I distinctly remember he had a salad containing tomatoes with his main course.

'Any joy?' asked Sam as I returned to her side.

'The only common link I can find are raw tomatoes, but beyond that I haven't a clue what, who, why or how.'

'I think I know how' said Sam. 'Well at least I'm pretty sure I do, in that I'm fairly certain what poison has been used. The only poison that acts as fast as this to my knowledge is cyanide, at least, I don't know of any others that act this quickly.'

'Look there's nothing we can do here' I

said. 'I'll just check with the police and see if we can leave. I don't know about you, but I'm completely knackered.'

I gave the police our details, including our hotel and room number and they let us leave. We caught a cab back to the hotel and were thankfully asleep by 1.00 am.

Chapter Two

As we both slept and totally unbeknown to us, Gemma Borgert who was staying in a Paris hotel two miles away from Sam and I, got dressed for a lone night time walk. She wore a black polo neck jumper over a pair of denim jeans and on top of those she put on her camel coloured overcoat and a black headscarf, and then finally pulling on a pair of black leather gloves she walked out of the hotel and headed for the offices of 'Le Figaro'. The head office of Frances's largest circulation right wing daily newspaper is located at 14 Boulevard Haussmann, and twelve minutes later Gemma arrived outside the main entrance.

Gemma could see what was going on inside the reception area through the glass doors, and like all daily newspapers around the world 'La

Figaro' ran a twenty four hours a day operation. Gemma could see there was just one receptionist on duty at 2.00 am in the morning, and she patiently waited for the receptionist to get totally engrossed dealing with somebody else. Wearing a pair of large lensed sunglasses which hid most of her face, Gemma stooped quite low and then using a walking stick she slowly headed through the main door, and without speaking to a soul she left a large A4 sized brown envelope on the reception desk, and turned to leave.

The envelope was addressed in large block capital letters to 'THE EDITOR' and in red ink beneath his title it said 'EXTREMELY URGENT'. Having left the envelope, Gemma quietly walked out using the same characteristic stoop, again aided by her walking stick. She knew her visit to 'Le Figaro' had certainly been un-noticed by anyone present in the foyer, but she hoped it had also been unseen by any CCTV cameras, but then she realised, even if she had been caught on camera, they wouldn't recognize her or be able to accurately describe her as all they would see was a doddery old lady wearing a headscarf and dark sunglasses. Gemma returned to her hotel, had a shower and then tried to get a good night's sleep.

The current editor of 'Le Figaro' was Oscar Dubois. He had been the editor now for nearly two years having previously been a freelance journalist for many years before becoming a reporter and then the Chief reporter for 'L'Opinion', a classical liberal daily newspaper. After three years Oscar left when he was offered the post of editor at 'Le Monde', a centre left daily newspaper. But becoming the editor of 'Le Figaro', the largest circulation daily newspaper in France was every French journalists ultimate aim, even if it meant being incredibly flexible over your own personal politics. Gemma's envelope duly arrived on the editor's desk about fifteen minutes after she had left it on the receptionists counter. Oscar carefully opened it, having had it checked by security to see if it contained a bomb. Having got the all clear Oscar pulled out a single sheet of plain white A4 size paper. It read as follows:

To the people of Paris

I, Mrs Borgert did last night poison and hopefully kill, several customers at an upmarket Parisian restaurant of my choice. I do not know or care how many people were killed and however many did die last night, well I'm afraid it wasn't be enough. It is my firm intention to continue with my campaign of

poisoning the people of Paris until I feel my need for
revenge on Paris has been fully satisfied.
I want the people of Paris to know exactly what I did,
and how easy it was, and so I have decided to use this
newspaper as my way of informing you. I took my
opportunity when a delivery truck of fresh fruit and
vegetables was left unattended for a couple of
minutes, while its driver made a delivery inside the
restaurant. While he was delivering produce inside I
injected a small amount of liquid cyanide into several
of the fresh tomatoes waiting on the trucks tailgate to
be delivered to the restaurant.
So be warned - my revenge on Paris has begun, and it
will not cease until I am satisfied.

The letter was dramatically signed 'Mrs Borgert'
using red ink, the same colour and shade as
dried blood. Oscar read it through to himself
again, then shouted to his news editor

'Pierre, this may sound a bit weird, but
have you heard anything about a mass
poisoning in a Paris restaurant tonight?'

'No, nothing' he replied.

'Well give the police a call and find out.
I've got a letter here from some mad woman
claiming she's set on poisoning half of Paris, and
she says she started tonight at a Paris
restaurant.'

'Sounds like a crank to me. Forget it Oscar.'

'Well do me a favour Pierre and satisfy my undying curiosity. If it is genuine then we've got a great scoop on our hands'.

Pierre picked up the phone on his desk and rang his usual contact at the police headquarters located at 71 Rue Albert in the 13th arrondissement. He spoke quietly for about three minutes then slowly replaced the receiver. Pierre looked up;

'Bloody hell Oscar, it's only bloody well true. Seven people have been pronounced dead, all poisoned this evening in the same restaurant, Michelle Andre's place 'Cuisine Raffinée' on the Champs-Élysées. The police reckon it's definitely deliberate.'

'Too right it's deliberate' said the Editor 'and unlike the police, 'Le Figaro' knows exactly who did it and how they did it. Give me a hand to put this together Pierre and for the moment let's keep it to just the two of us. I've got a new headline and a great new story for tomorrow's front page.

Chapter Three

Sam and I woke up the following morning and

as we drank our morning cup of tea we switched on the TV to see if there was any mention of the restaurant poisonings. Never mind a mention, the broadcast media had gone mad. Every channel was featuring the same story, mainly thanks to this morning's very dramatic headline in 'Le Figaro' which read 'Restaurant de la mort' or in English 'Restaurant of Death'.

Mrs Borgert's letter to the people of Paris had been reproduced as a large 'blow up' version on the front page of 'Le Figaro', and Paris was already running scared, or at least, so the TV channels were saying.

'So who is this Mrs Borgert' asked Sam 'and revenge for what?'

'No idea love' I replied 'but I'd like to find out. Apart from murdering seven innocent people who she obviously didn't know, she totally screwed up our second wedding anniversary celebration'.

'What I don't get' said Sam thinking out loud as she spoke 'is her name. Mrs Borgert sounds sort of European, possibly Austrian, Swiss or German, but if that's the case why did she write her letter in English?'

'Mmm' I muttered. 'That's interesting. While you were speaking I looked up the surname Borgert on the internet, and according to this particular website it says the family name of Borgert shows up principally in six different countries, although I would think there must be a few Borgert's all over the world'.

'So which are the six countries?' asked Sam.

'35% of Borgert's apparently live in the USA' I answered reading from my laptop. '24% are in Brazil, 15% in Germany, 11% in Sweden, 8% in Argentina and 2% here in France. As far as I can see from this, there are none in the UK, so why is the letter in English?'

'Well if 35% of Borgert's live in America, I guess that's a good starting point, after all, Americans speak English'.

'Mmm, that's a debateable point' I muttered.

'Anyway' said Sam 'there's not much we can do about it. The French police we know from past experience don't take very kindly to Interpol interfering, besides which we're here on a brief holiday, not to work'.

'Oh I know that love' I replied 'but with our experience and our knowledge of poisons from our run-ins with the terrorists in Cairo, I think we could really help, particularly if this Mrs Borgert woman is intent on murdering more people. I mean you told me within half an hour that it was more than likely Cyanide poisoning, and I felt from my brief look round the restaurant at the common food link that it was probably tomatoes. You and I realised both of those things within thirty minutes, which was several hours before the police. We both have good instincts and good knowledge, and to be honest Sam, I'd like to stay on in Paris awhile and see what we can find out, purely unofficial of course.'

'Well I suppose we could stay on a few days' replied Sam 'and see if we can come up with anything, but don't then blame me if the French police deport us for interfering in their case'.

'Wouldn't dream of it Mrs Turner'. I said smiling.

Chapter Four

Gemma was very pleased with her initial achievement, as that was how she saw it. Paris had killed her husband with their 'we're better than you' attitude to life and their completely lackadaisical attitudes to food hygiene and basic health and safety.
Seven dead was a good start, but it was nowhere near enough to satisfy her need for revenge.

Gemma realised that she would need to stay in Paris if she was to continue with her plans, but most importantly if she was not going to get caught, then she had to get out of her Mrs Borgert mind-set and once again become the extremely genteel and elegant Lady Louise Hamilton Smythe.

The first thing to do was move to a more suitable hotel where she could base herself for the duration of the task she had set herself, and ensure that she was seen to be the perfect aristocratic English lady doing all the things aristocratic genteel ladies do when abroad. Take afternoon tea, attend classical music concerts, go to the ballet and the theatre etc. After all, she had done all those things most of her adult life anyway. The first job then was to book into a suitable hotel. After a fairly lengthy internet search she finally decided on the 'Four Seasons Hotel George V, Paris'. She didn't know the hotel, but reading the description on its website she decided its 'palatial comfort, exquisite old-world refinement and the most extravagant flower arrangements in the city sums up this historic hotel by the Champs-Elysées. Paired with its dazzling mirage of aristocratic Paris is a gastronomic galaxy of stars across its three

Michelin restaurants and a new spa with champagne bar'. The section of description that clinched it for her was 'In a wide avenue off the celebrity Champs-Elysées in the upmarket 8e arrondissement. Shops - both mainstream megastores and haute-couture fashion boutiques - hem in the hotel on all sides, but then, this is the illustrious Golden Triangle with the crème de la crème of fashion houses'. Having made her decision Gemma picked up her mobile and dialled the number. It was answered by a very polite gentlemen's voice after the first ring.

'Bonjour, Quatre saisons le roi Cinquime' which not speaking French Gemma assumed meant 'Good morning, Four Seasons Hotel George V'.

'Good morning' she answered.

'Ah, good morning madam' replied the voice immediately switching to speak in perfect English without a trace of accent.

'This is Lady Louise Hamilton Smythe, and I shall require a suite of rooms for at least a month, possibly longer. Can your establishment assist me in this?'

'Of course my lady, it will be our pleasure'.

I bet it will at the prices you charge she thought to herself.

'If I may ask' continued the receptionist 'from what date would your ladyship require the suite, and what size of suite would most suit your needs?'

'I wish to entertain, and so I will require at least two large reception rooms, and I would like to arrive within the hour if that would be possible?'

'Of course my lady' he said 'we have an excellent suite of the size you require on the fourth floor and it will be available for you whenever you choose to arrive. I will have some fresh flowers put in all the rooms for you immediately. Is there anything else you will require at this stage my lady?'

'That will be all thank you' said Gemma in her best Lady Louise voice and with that she put the phone down. She checked out of the fairly basic and anonymous hotel room she had booked into for the past twenty four hours, and ordering a taxi she headed off with all her luggage for the Four Seasons Hotel George V, Paris.

Gemma settled leisurely into her suite at the hotel and decided the next hour or so should be spent on deciding who her next victims were going to be, and how would she go about poisoning them? It had to be poison as that's what had killed Matthias, he'd been poisoned. Gemma eventually decided her next victims should be doctors, and thinking about it she realised the only place she'd find lots of doctors in one place was a hospital. Using a website search engine again, much to her surprise Gemma discovered that the Assistance Publique Hôpitaux de Paris was rated the number one hospital in the whole of Europe. That was good enough for Gemma, it would be full of doctors worth killing. The next question was how? She didn't want to use cyanide again, so she sat and thought through her various options.

Option one was arsenic. Arsenic had been known as an effective poison since Roman times and it had been used to poison all manner of rivals and even emperors. One of the favourite versions was what is known as white arsenic, or arsenic oxide. It is a water-soluble, tasteless solid, and is easily added to drinks. Since the 1800's various arsenic compounds had become widely available, and were now used in all manner of easily purchasable products such as weed-killers, flypapers, rat poisons etc, and of course arsenic had been used in numerous domestic murders, both in the real world and in the world of fictional murders. It was Agatha Christie's poison of choice.

Gemma's second option was atropine, or as it's more commonly known, belladonna. This particular poison is extracted from the juice of the berries of the deadly nightshade bush, and in small doses atropine causes hallucinations and was used for this purpose as long ago as ancient Greece. In larger doses it was reputed to be one of the favourite poisons of would-be murderers in Medieval Europe as the juice of a few berries only is all that's needed to make it fatal.

A third possibility Gemma considered was strychnine which can be extracted from the seeds of the nux vomica tree, which sadly for her purposes only grows in Southeast Asia. However, strychnine became widely available in the west as trade with the Far East expanded, and it was reputed to be an excellent tonic and when prescribed in small doses it was said by doctors to greatly aid convalescence. It is also widely used to poison rats and other animals and as such is easily obtained, and Gemma felt sure that although it had been cited in only a few domestic murders, its ready availability suggested to her that it had probably been used in many murders.

The final poison Gemma was considering was Thallium. This element was only discovered in the 1860s and while it has been used in several domestic murders, Gemma was fully aware that it has been more widely used as an extremely effective method of assassination across the world, and in this context it would be ideal for Gemma's purposes. Thallium sulphate is water-soluble and is completely tasteless, but best of all it takes several days for the symptoms to appear, and even then these are generally attributed to other illnesses. Gemma remembered reading during her medical studies at Oxford that thallium was used by both Saddam Hussein's secret police and by the Russian assassins of the KGB. She decided 'If was good enough for them it was good enough for her'. So thallium it was. Now, how to get hold of it?'

Gemma searched online and found several companies selling thallium in various forms, but because of the nature of the product they all required certification from an official research lab or something similar. However, there was one supplier based in Bulgaria that would ship her exactly what she wanted with no questions asked. They charged nearly six times what the legitimate companies charged, but money didn't matter, and thanks to her father's generosity regarding his only daughter, money was never going to be a problem. Gemma left the hotel, found the nearest post office, obtained the key to the French version of a PO Box, and then returning to the hotel she went back on line to the supplier in Bulgaria, purchased what she needed and had it sent to her new PO Box in the centre of Paris. Now she had to wait for her parcel to arrive in her PO Box, but Gemma decided she would use that time to ingratiate herself into Paris society as the very genteel, butter wouldn't melt in her mouth Lady Louise Hamilton Smythe.

Chapter Five

I woke up with a low to medium grade headache, and very unfairly I thought, Sam apparently felt completely fine. We'd both had a very pleasant meal at our hotel's restaurant, eventually deciding we had to eat somewhere and our own hotel was probably as safe as anywhere else, and to accompany the meal we had got through two bottles of a very good Merlot. Although if I'm honest and in all fairness, I had drunk most of it apart from the two glasses Sam had drunk, so the headache was in all probability nobody's fault but my own.

'Come on you' commanded Sam 'get out of that bed, shower and dress and then let's go and get breakfast, I'm starving'.

'You're a cruel, cruel woman Mrs Turner' I commented, but then I meekly did as requested, feeling it would be quite unfair to punish Sam for my excessive wine consumption and the resulting headache.

Sitting at a quiet table in the corner of the hotel's restaurant, we talked about what we could do to try and trace Mrs Borgert.

'The obvious place to start' said Sam 'is with the French Borgert's as this is happening in France, and I guess if there's no joy there we start ploughing through other records. Do you think Helena would let us use Interpol's computer records as this is not an Interpol matter?'

'I don't see why not' I answered. 'After all, it's in everybody's interest to find this woman and stop her from murdering anybody else, and like it or not France is part of Europe and therefore it comes under Interpol'.

Helena was Chief Superintendent Helena Van Houten, Interpol's Head of European

Operations. Whenever we were working with Interpol, which we did on a part time consulting basis, Helena was our boss, and she had also over the years become one of our best friends, even to the extent that she was Sam's principal bridesmaid at our wedding two years earlier.

'I'll ring her' said Sam dialling Helena's number.

After a minute or two of catching up on personal matters, Sam explained about our being at the restaurant and having witnessed all seven deaths, and that we were keen to see if we could help, but without letting the French police know as we didn't want to rock the boat by trying to poke our nose in officially. Helena agreed with our 'behind the scenes' approach and offered to get a couple of her Interpol staff back at Interpol's HQ searching the computer database for any Borgert's that may have a connection, however loose.

'Well that saves us time and effort trawling through records' said Sam filling me in, 'and Helena also sends you her love by the way'.

'So what do we do now?' I asked Sam.

'Well, we usually try and put ourselves in the position of the person we are trying to find, and try to think like they may be thinking, if that makes any sense?'

'Yes, I get it' I replied. 'So if we were trying to get revenge, for whatever reason, the next step is to poison more people, but who, where, when and how?'

'Haven't a clue' said Sam 'but let's try thinking about it'.

'Well, we've no idea about the 'who' as her victims seem to be random, so let's forget the 'who' for the moment.'

'Agreed' said Sam.

'Next, where?' I asked.

'Well if she's going to poison people as she stated in her letter' said Sam 'then I guess it has to be places where they eat, ie restaurants or cafes. Although it could be via baker's shops, butchers, supermarkets, or perhaps works canteens or… Oh God, it could be anywhere. So let's forget the 'where' for the moment.

'OK, fine. So what about when?' I asked.

'Forget that as well' replied Sam. 'It could be later today, tomorrow, next week or next month. Let's be honest, we haven't a clue about any of this.'

'Yes we do' I said. We should work on the how, and if she's going to poison people she'll obviously need poison.'

'My God' said Sam 'I've married a genius. Case solved then!'

'Oh shut up dearest' I said laughing. 'Seriously, between us we know a hell of a lot about poison from that dreadful Madam Favreau during the Cairo Conspiracy.

'True' said Sam. 'OK, well in that case I go back to what I said when we were at the 'restaurant of death' as Le Figaro insisted on calling it, as far as I'm aware cyanide is the only poison that acts that fast.'

'Yes, true, and I agree with you, but what if she's not bothered about speed from now on? She's made her big announcement with the seven restaurant deaths and the letter to Le Figaro, and if I was her I'd now take my time and dream up all sorts of ways of poisoning whoever it is she wants to poison. Plus, I'd certainly want to change my 'modus operandi' so that there's no pattern for the police to follow and therefore more chance of getting away with it.'

'Mmm' mused Sam. 'I see your point, and it makes a lot of sense. OK, so let's put our minds to various poisons and their effects, and also ease of availability, because as we both know, really effective poisons aren't that easily available.'

How wrong we were.

Chapter Six

Lady Louise Hamilton Smythe was holding court to a room full of invited guests in her suite of rooms at the Four Seasons Hotel George V. The previous evening she had attended the ballet, at the famous Palais Garnier, generally considered to be one of the most important buildings in all of Paris. Seating 1,979 patrons the Palais Garnier is also one of the largest theatres in the world, and certainly one of the most lavish in its design. Lady Louise had decided she needed to announce herself in Paris and chose to do so by attending a performance of William Shakespeare's play 'Romeo and Juliet' which had been transformed into a stunning ballet with beautiful music by Sergei Prokofiev and had first been performed in Czechoslovakia in 1938.

During the interval Lady Louise carefully chose several ladies around her own age, and after chatting with them over a glass of champagne she invited them to share afternoon tea with her the following day in her suite at the Four Seasons George V.

The hotel did her proud laying on two varieties of tea, both Lapsang souchong and Earl Grey, along with a wonderful array of sandwiches, cakes and pastries, all neatly arrayed on top quality porcelain. Lady Louise had even asked the hotel to provide three waiters for the afternoon, which they happily did for an exorbitant fee, but she didn't mind the extra expense if it helped make the right impression. Lady Louise was her most welcoming and demur self that afternoon, making sure everyone knew just how cultured and genteel this sophisticated and aristocratic English damsel was, and after two hours she was convinced that nobody in their right mind would ever suspect her of being the Paris Poisoner.

Having worked really hard on making the right impression for the last three hours, Louise was greatly relieved to eventually get rid of all her dreadful guests. She really didn't warm to any of them and considered them all to be a pretentious waste of space, but 'needs must' as the saying goes. She quickly changed into casual clothes and suddenly she immediately felt like Gemma again, and not Lady Louise. It was strange and uncanny, but she realised that what she wore had a massive effect on her mind-set. Most unexpected and strange, but nevertheless true and worth remembering. She hurriedly made her way to the post office aiming to get there before it closed. Arriving just in time she was thrilled to see a large brown padded envelope waiting for collection in her PO Box. She put the envelope in the large shopping bag she was carrying and quickly made her way back to the hotel.

Thallium sulphate was used for various medical treatments for over two hundred years, but for various reasons its use in medicine was abandoned. Thallium sulphate is soluble in water and its toxic effects means a lethal dose of for an adult is just one gram. Since thallium sulphate is a simple powder with indistinctive properties, it can easily be mistaken for more innocuous chemicals, and it can enter the human body by various means such as ingestion, inhalation, or even simple contact with the skin. Due to its poisonous nature, many western countries have banned it as a dosage as small as 500 mg has been reported as fatal. After it has entered the body, Thallium sulphate concentrates itself in the kidneys, liver, brain, and other tissues in the body. It is a very slow and extremely painful death which usually takes about four days from initial ingestion. Having studied and obtained a degree in medicine at Oxford University, Lady Louise, or Gemma as she was currently thinking of herself knew all this, and she thought the possibilities were both endless and exiting.

Gemma had already decided that her next targets were going to be doctors. After all, it was a doctor that had completely let her down the most in her time of need when poor Matthias needed their help. Having done most of her research online, Gemma discovered that 'Assistance Publique - Hôpitaux de Paris' was in fact the university hospital trust operating in Paris and its surroundings. It was also the largest hospital system in Europe and one of the largest in the world, not only providing health care, but also teaching, research, prevention, education and emergency medical service in fifty two different branches of medicine. Employing more than 90,000 people, which included 15,800 doctors in 44 hospitals, it would make the perfect target. Gemma decided she needed to target a specific hospital, and she eventually settled on a teaching hospital in the 13th arrondissement of Paris. Her chosen hospital was part of the 'Assistance Publique Hôpitaux de Paris', with Pitie-Salptriere University Hospital' not only being a large teaching hospital, it was also the incredibly prestigious teaching hospital of the Sorbonne University, and one of Europe's largest hospital. It was also France's largest hospital and Gemma was sure they would have plenty of doctors to kill.

Chapter Seven

Helena had just telephoned Sam back and informed her that there were thousands of Borgert's spread around the world, but none of them jumped out as being in the least bit suspicious, and she had no useful suggestions to make to aid our search.

'OK, so no joy there then' I said. 'Any suggestions?'

'Look' said Sam 'My thinking is that if she is going to continue with her plan to poison people here in Paris, then there's a ninety nine percent chance that she's holed up here in Paris somewhere, probably in a hotel or guest house'.

Yeah, I agree' I replied 'and that makes perfect sense. But surely she wouldn't register in a hotel as Mrs Borgert, she'd have to be using a false passport or ID card.'

'So where would she get a false passport?' asked Sam.

'Supposing it's not a false passport?' I asked. Look, in her letter to Le Figaro she signed herself Mrs Borgert, which means she's married?'

'Agreed' said Sam 'but so what. How does that help?'

'Supposing she's still got a passport in her maiden name and is using that?'

'Oh great Sherlock' sighed Sam. 'So now we're looking for a woman whose name is completely unknown to us. Really helpful dearest?'

'In fairness to me' I responded 'I didn't say it was helpful in finding her, but that it may be how she is avoiding detection. You and I both know the police will have checked out every Mrs Borgert staying in Paris the minute they read her letter in Le Figaro.'

'I hate to say this' said Sam ' but I think the only chance we or the police stand is if she strikes again and leaves some kind of clue. At the moment I'm afraid we're all floundering in the dark.'

Two days later and unbeknown to the two of us, the Paris Poisoner was based in the same area of Paris as ourselves. Gemma Borgert was a registered guest under her maiden name of Lady Louise Hamilton Smythe in a luxury suite of rooms at the Four Seasons Hotel George V on

Avenue George V, and Sam and I had a very comfortable double room in the Hotel Chateau Frontenac on 54 Rue Pierre Charron, just two streets away.

Gemma was very busy on that morning having prepared two syringes of Thallium the night before. She left the hotel around 10.30 am with both syringes residing in an otherwise empty hard spectacle case which was itself lying in her handbag. She arrived at the hospital and was pleased to see it was incredibly busy with hundreds of people coming and going. Knowing hospitals as well as she did from her time as a student at Oxford where she had spent many a week in hospitals, she knew hospital routines and assumed French hospitals would work on more or less similar lines to a UK hospital in that doctors usually had their own changing rooms. Gemma's grasp of French was very limited, but she had looked up various key words and phrases she might need on Google translate before setting off, and she knew that she would find the doctor's changing rooms on a door signed 'Médecins Vestiaire'. Gemma wandered around the corridors and after ten minutes she found the door she was looking for. She glanced around to see if anyone was watching her, but nobody was, so she knocked on the door and without waiting for a reply she opened it and walked in. She had a story ready, but it wasn't necessary as the room was empty. She searched round the room and eventually found what she wanted behind a plain cabinet door in a cupboard next to the sink. A fridge. She opened it, and inside were several different plastic containers of food, a couple of yogurts, a cardboard box of pastries and one or two sandwiches simply wrapped up in clingfilm. She quickly walked over to the door of the room and locked it with the key that had fortunately been left in the lock. Returning to the fridge she then removed each item of food, and then very carefully and methodically injected the contents of the two syringes into each of the pastries, all of the sandwiches and through the lids of the two yogurts. Gemma hoped the owners of the yogurts would not notice the tiny holes in the lids, but the syringes were incredibly thin, so she thought it was unlikely. In total it took just four minutes to empty both syringes of thallium which she then put back into the glasses case in her hand bag. Checking everything was back in the fridge just as she'd found it, she unlocked the door, opened it and walked out into the corridor, down the stairs and then out of the hospital.

Nothing happened for twenty four hours, and Gemma wasn't surprised by that. The effects of thallium were very different to cyanide and she knew it would take time. The first doctor to complain of not feeling well was Doctor Malcolm Fitzpatrick, a gynaecologist at the hospital. He initially started vomiting along with a pretty severe case of diarrhoea. This not only continued during the next twenty four hours, but the severity greatly increased, and he also noticed his hair was starting to fall out. He had by now been admitted as a patient in his own hospital, and the doctor treating him became suspicious when Dr Fitzpatrick started having problems with several of his main organs. His lungs were not functioning at full capacity, his heart started fluttering and both his liver and his kidneys started to shut down. The following day Dr Malcolm Fitzpatrick died having been diagnosed with thallium poisoning. During the time of Dr Fitzpatrick's illness three other doctors from the hospital had failed to report for work and after Mrs Borgert's very public threats the police were now very suspicious. Their investigations over the next couple of days convinced the Chief detective that the Paris Poisoner, the elusive Mrs Borgert, had struck again.

By the end of the week, four of Paris's best doctors were dead. Le Figaro had already picked up on the death of Dr Fitzpatrick and one of their reporters had discovered from chatting up several nurses at the hospital where Dr Fitzpatrick had worked, that there were in fact four dead doctors and they had all been poisoned with thallium. His editor knew what he was about to do was unfair, but he could smell massive circulation increases, and that would thrill the publisher and greatly enhance his standing at the paper. So the following days headline in Le Figaro was blunt and to the point, as Oscar Dubois had decided to use the title of an old Elton John song from his 'Caribou' album:

'THE BITCH IS BACK'

'That heartless bitch Mrs Borgert has struck again, this time killing four of our most wonderful doctors. Is nobody safe from this horrendous woman, and what are our useless police doing to protect the people of Paris?'

He knew it was unfair on the police, but as he saw it he was just doing his job.

Gemma had a copy of both 'Le Figaro' and 'La

Monde' delivered to her suite every day to keep up to date with what was being said about her, and with the aid of some excellent scanning and translation software on her laptop she was able to read what was being printed by Le Figaro in English. Excellent she thought, they hate me as much as I hate them. Time to respond I think, and with that Gemma sat down to compose a second letter to Le Figaro.

Chapter Eight

Gemma had finished her letter and she was very pleased with the finished result. However, having thought about it she decided she needed to change the method of delivery to Le Figaro. It was far too risky to walk through the door and deliver it personally herself. Having thought about it for a while she had narrowed her choices down to two options. One, go to the area of Le Figaro's offices and ask a passing child to deliver it in exchange for a cash payment, or two, drop it off at a courier's office and get them to deliver it. She preferred using the child option as they were far more innocent, and most French children if they were anything like their English counterparts would do anything for a few Euros. She needed to disguise herself a bit but it was not her strong point. However, before trying to find a suitable child to do her dirty work she decided she would need to do a bit of shopping, and so Gemma went out that morning and after two hours of searching she had made her five purchases. A medium length good quality grey wig from a local hair salon, a tatty second hand dress that looked as if it came from the 1950's, a suitably old thick knit dark green cardigan, a pair of dark brown ladies shoes in a style she normally wouldn't be seen dead in, and lastly an old and well used walking stick, the last four items all bought from a second hand charity shop. Having completed her purchases Gemma returned to the hotel and locked herself in her bedroom. She stripped down to her underwear and firstly put on the dress which was in a dark grey thick material and was covered in a pattern of green leaves and red flowers. The charity shop had obviously cleaned it and although it looked old it both smelt and felt fresh. She put on the cardigan, which was a bit big for her, but that didn't matter. She'd already tried the shoes in the charity shop and as she slipped them on she knew they would fit her OK, and so lastly she put the grey wig on over her own hair. The transformation was completed with her large sunglasses. She didn't recognize the person staring back at her, and she knew it would work. She quickly took everything off and dumped it all in a large shopping bag she had, along with the letter for the editor of Le Figaro, who she now knew was a certain Oscar Dubois. Dressing in her own clothes again and picking up the shopping bag, she left the hotel and headed towards the offices of Le Figaro. Once in the area she started searching the back streets, where she eventually found what she wanted - a run-down guest house with several rooms to let. Gemma walked in and found the proprietor smoking a cigarette in the back garden. Offering the man cash, Gemma acquired a small room on the first floor for which she paid him a month in advance. The proprietor asked for no identification and she offered none. She took the key from him, immediately went up the stairs and went into the room. It was small and dingy with a single bed, a small wardrobe and a small chest of drawers. The bathroom she discovered was shared by everyone on that floor. Gemma got changed into the charity shop clothes leaving her own inside the small wardrobe, put on the wig and sunglasses, picked up her shopping bag containing the letter, and clutching her walking stick, she quietly as possible crept down the stairs. The proprietor was still in the back garden and Gemma managed to leave the building without being seen by him or anyone else. She immediately adopted a stooped position and walked very slowly using the walking stick. She got to the road junction with the offices of Le Figaro in front of her, but on the other side of the road. Gemma stood back and watched as people walked by, and after what felt like an hour, but was in reality just eleven minutes, she saw a boy aged about ten or eleven walking towards her. She had a phrase in French ready to use and as the boy got closer she indicated with her walking stick that she wanted to speak to him. He walked over to her and politely said:

'Bonjour madam'.

Gemma replied with her prepared phrase in French:

'Pouvez-vous s'il vous plait livrer cette letter pour moi. Je te donnerai dix euros'. Which as far as she knew meant in English 'Can you please deliver this letter for me. I will give you ten euros'.

The boy obviously understood her as she held out the letter and a ten euro note and pointed to the offices of Le Figaro across the road with her walking stick. The boy shrugged his shoulders, grabbed the letter and the ten euro note and dodging between the cars successfully crossed the road. He disappeared inside the offices of the newspaper and re-emerged empty handed back on the street just over a minute later. Gemma immediately walked away and disappeared down the back streets returning to her rented room. There she got changed leaving the old clothes, the shoes, the walking stick and the wig in the wardrobe, and dressed again in her own clothes she quietly left the building and decided she'd take a leisurely walk back to her hotel. Mission accomplished.

Chapter Nine

Oscar Dubois was in the briefing room discussing ideas and other possible stories with all his day-time reporters when the boy from the post department dropped about twenty envelopes on his desk. Among them was a large A4 sized white envelope addressed to Monsieur Oscar Dubois, Editor, Le Figaro. The letters sat on his desk for over forty minutes before he eventually finished his meeting, sat down again and started working his way through the post. He opened the envelope and pulled out the single sheet of white paper. It read:

Monsieur Oscar Dubois

Editor
Le Figaro

To the people of Paris

As you will have realised by now I have taken another step in my ongoing need for revenge against the people of Paris. However, I feel I must point out that the editor of Le Figaro has been most unkind to me as I do not take kindly to being referred to as 'the bitch'. Be assured Monsieur Dubois, for the use of those two badly chosen words I am now very seriously considering adding you to my list, and I now give you full warning that unless you start to show some understanding of my suffering I will make you the last of my future victims to die. Of course that will only be once my revenge has been completed and you as my means of addressing the people of Paris have served your purpose.

Why four doctors you may ask? Well to be honest, yet again I didn't know how many doctors or indeed which doctors would die, but it really doesn't matter. When I desperately needed their help, the medical profession of Paris along with other professions let me down badly, and I do not and cannot forgive or forget easily. As the police will know by now, on this occasion I chose to use thallium injected into their packed lunches, as I am fully aware that thallium

causes intolerable pain and suffering which to me
seemed most appropriate.
Be aware Paris, be very aware. I have barely started.

Again, the letter was signed 'Mrs Borgert' using
the same shade of dark red ink.

Oscar Dubois showed the letter to Pierre.

'Bloody hell Oscar' he said 'She's really
taken a dislike to your headline. What are you
going to do?'

'I'm going to print it on the front page
again' said Oscar 'but thinking about it I'll leave
out the bit about me. That's quite personal and it
doesn't affect the readers. Type it up for
tomorrow's edition please Pierre, and then give
me a few possible headlines to choose from,
although my initial instinct is to run with the last
line of her letter.'

'Be aware Paris, be very aware, I have
barely started' he said 'Yeah, I like it Oscar, let's
go with that. I assume we need to give the
original to the police again, but like the first
letter I don't suppose they'll find any
fingerprints other than yours and mine.'

The police didn't, and when Detective Chief
Inspector Claude Moreau interrogated the front

desk receptionist about who delivered the letter, the man on the front desk told him it was a boy aged about ten who told him it was from a crippled old lady across the main road who had asked him to deliver it. Nobody other than the boy had seen the old woman and nobody knew who the boy was. DCI Moreau was getting incredibly frustrated with the whole case. He'd now got eleven dead bodies in the city morgue, mounting pressure from his political masters, and as he said to his team of detectives;

'The trouble is nobody knows who this Mrs Borgert is, nobody knows where Mrs Borgert is, nobody knows why Mrs Borgert wants revenge and nobody has the vaguest idea what Mrs Borgert wants revenge for.

I picked up the following mornings edition of Le Figaro, and although my French was pretty useless I understood the bold headline printed in red capital letters.
SOYEZ CONSCIENT PARIS, SOYEZ TRES CONSCIENT. L'AI A PEINE COMMENCÉ.
Sam, who's French was much better than mine confirmed that it said
BE AWARE PARIS, BE VERY AWARE. I HAVE BARELY STARTED.
There then followed her latest letter, but unbeknown to us at that stage minus the threat

she had made about Oscar Dubois.

'Good grief' said Sam 'Four doctors murdered. Why on earth would anyone want to kill four doctors? All we ever try to do as doctors is good and more than anything try to save people's lives. What on earth has she got against doctors?'

'Perhaps that's it' I said. 'You may have unwittingly hit the nail on the head. Look, in her letter she says *'When I desperately needed their help, the medical profession of Paris along with other professions let me down badly, and I do not and cannot forgive or forget easily.'* Perhaps doctors failed to save the life of someone who was really close to her, a good friend or a relative, and in her grief she feels doctors let her down and so she is taking it out on anyone she can, including doctors?'

'That makes sense' said Sam 'but if you're right I can't see someone getting this worked up over the death of a friend, however close they were, no, it has to be someone really close to warrant murdering eleven people as revenge.'

'Well she always signs herself Mrs Borgert, perhaps Mr Borgert died?'

'Good thinking and you could be right, but how the hell do we find out?'

Chapter Ten

Gemma had rested at the hotel when she had first got back from her murderous trip to the hospital two days ago, and now she had changed into clothes more appropriate for her Lady Louise persona. It was really strange she thought to herself, when I dress in casual clothes, jumpers, sweat shirts, jeans or slacks etc, the sort of clothes myself and Matthias relaxed together in, I automatically become Gemma and I constantly feel this tremendous pain. But when I dress as Lady Louise in smart dresses, elegant trouser suits and put on expensive jewellery, it's as if I suddenly become another person, someone that doesn't feel that pain. Well at least, not to the same extent.

She was about to call for a pot of coffee to be sent up when the telephone in her hotel suite rang.

'Ah, bonjour Mademoiselle Lady Hamilton Smythe', said a man's voice she was not familiar with. 'My name is Henri Le Grande, and I am the head concierge here at the hotel.'

'Good morning Monsieur Le Grande, and what can I do for you?' she asked.

'It is more a case of what I can do for you

Mademoiselle, if you will permit me to explain. As the head concierge of Paris's most prestigious hotel I am frequently given 'first refusal' as you English say on tickets for various very exclusive events. One such event is happening tomorrow at the Louvre, when the largest collection of known paintings by the great Italian master Canaletto, including several from many royal and private collections not seen before, will all be on display for a private viewing by selected guests.'

'Continue' commanded Lady Louise.

'I am aware of your ladyship's love of the arts, and I would like to offer you a pair of those exclusive tickets. They are of course totally free of charge, but however should you wish to make a donation to any of the wonderful charities supported by the Louvre then it would of course be greatly appreciated. Only the best champagne and canapés will be served by liveried waiters and I trust you do not think me presumptuous in making this offer.'

'Indeed not Monsieur Le Grande, I am most grateful to you and I will happily accept one of your tickets. As you may know, I am here in Paris on my own and have yet to find a suitable companion for such an event. I trust one ticket is acceptable to you, and if so, what time does the exhibition commence?'

'I will have a ticket sent to your suite immediately Mademoiselle, and the exhibition opens to invited guests at 11.00 am and to the public at 12 noon. I trust you will have a most enjoyable and pleasant time at the Louvre.'

Lady Louise returned the telephone to its cradle and made a note in her diary so that she wouldn't forget the start time. She had studied 'A' level art at Cheltenham Ladies College, and she was both familiar with Canaletto's work and fond of the accurate architectural detail he incorporated in his paintings. Canaletto's real name was Giovanni Antonio Canal, but he was known by everyone as Canaletto. He was born in Venice and during his lifetime he painted hundreds of views of Venice, Rome and London. Lady Louise remembered reading some time ago that the record price paid at auction for a Canaletto was £18.6 million pounds at Sotheby's in London back in July 2005 for a view of the Grand Canal in Venice looking towards the Rialto. This she was sure would be an exhibition worth attending.

We were both to say the least getting frustrated at our lack of progress. We'd had this idea that

Mrs Borgert may be incredibly distressed over the death of a close relative, the most likely being her husband, and want revenge for whatever had happened to him. However, having checked it out Helena assured us there were no recorded deaths of a Mr Borgert in Paris, or for that matter in the whole of France in the last twelve months.

'Come on love' said Sam. 'Let's get our mind off it for a few hours and do something relaxing. How about a visit to a famous Parisian attraction. There's the Louvre, the Moulin Rouge or how about driving out to visit Versailles?'

'OK, but not Versailles' I said. 'It's not that I don't want to go, I do, but it needs planning and getting tickets in advance etc. The Moulin Rouge sounds fun but that's an evening thing really, isn't it?'

'In that case the Louvre it is' declared an excited Sam. 'I've always wanted to see Leonardo's Mona Lisa.'

'Why would anyone want to paint a picture of some woman called Lisa who just moans all the time?' I asked. 'The title says it all 'Moaner Lisa'.

'It's not spelt like that as you very well know' laughed Sam. 'I know you play the idiot a lot of the time, but I also happen to know that among your numerous qualifications you got a grade 1 A level in art. I came across all your old school and university certificates buried in a drawer when I was spring cleaning in the villa last year.'

'Yes, well as it happens I really would like to visit the Louvre. Apart from the Mona Lisa they also have several other Da Vinci's as well as the statue of the Venus de Milo, along with several works by Michelangelo, Raphael, Rembrandt and Caravaggio. I also saw a poster in the hotel's reception that there is a massive exhibition of Canaletto's opening today, and I'd really like to see those.'

'Good grief, my husband has just changed from a laid back part time crime solving detective and mystery thriller writer into a classical scholar before my very eyes. How the hell did that happen?' asked Sam with a grin on her face.

'Very funny dear' I smiled back. 'Look, I've always been into art, particularly the old masters, but I've never made a big thing of it. And let's be honest, we're not exactly awash with classical art galleries in the Algarve are we?'

'Good point' conceded Sam. 'OK Professor Turner, in that case I wish for you to give me an educational guided tour of the Louvre if you please.'

'Your wish is my command' I said bowing graciously.
We left for the Louvre five minutes later.

Chapter Eleven

We arrived at the Louvre just after 11.00 am and at my request we headed straight for the Canaletto exhibition. My thinking was that the Canaletto's would only be on display for a few days whereas the other artworks lived at the Louvre all the time.
Unfortunately when we arrived at the entrance to the exhibition we were informed by a uniformed guard that there was a private viewing for invited guests only taking place at the moment, but we were welcome to return at 12 noon. WE wandered off and spent the next hour wandering the galleries looking at some of the world's greatest masterpieces, including my first sight of the real 'Mona Lisa'. To be honest, I had never seen what all the fuss was about. For a start, and I apologize to the subject, but she's not exactly a raving beauty, she can't even smile properly and the horizon lines Leonardo has painted are different on either side of her. As I

say, I can't see what all the fuss is about, but then that's just my humble opinion. I looked at watch and noticed it was five minutes past twelve, so we returned to the entrance of the Canaletto exhibition, which was now open to the general public even though a lot of the invited guests were still milling around.

'Wow, now this is what I call a real artist' I said standing in front of a view of the Grand Canal in Venice. 'This is real quality, and I could stand and look at this for hours, you can keep your Mona Lisa.'

'I couldn't agree more' said a lady's voice behind me. I turned and saw a very elegant brunette aged I guessed in her late thirties or early forties, dressed in a dark blue trouser suit standing in front of me.

'I'm so sorry' she said. 'It was extremely rude of me to comment on a private conversation, but it was so good to hear an English voice amongst all this French babble, and particularly one who's thought processes coincided with mine.'
She held her hand out to shake and said;

'Good afternoon, I'm Lady Louise Hamilton Smythe and I was one of the fortunate guests to have been invited to the private viewing. I just love Canaletto.'

We both shook hands with her as I introduced us;

'Michael Turner and this is my wife Samantha'.

'Sam please' she said 'The only person that calls me Samantha is my mother whenever I've upset her or done something she doesn't approve of.'
Lady Louise laughed.

'So do you live here in Paris, or are you just visiting' she asked.

'No, we actually live in the Algarve region of Southern Portugal' I replied. 'We came initially for a long weekend to celebrate our second wedding anniversary, but it sort of got interrupted.'

'Why, what happened' she asked.

'We were having a very pleasant celebratory evening meal' said Sam 'at a top French restaurant named 'Cuisine Raffinée' on the Champs-Élysées, when suddenly people started dying all around us.'

'Oh my God' exclaimed Lady Louise. 'You were there when all those poor people were poisoned? How awful for you both.'

'To be honest' continued Sam 'yes it was horrid, but we were fine as we're sort of used to it. I used to be a police surgeon in the UK before we moved to the Algarve, and we both now do consultative work with Interpol'.

'I've lost count of the number of dead bodies we've seen in the last few years' I said, but I don't think my comment helped.

'Ooh, I don't think I could ever look at a dead body' replied Lady Louise. 'I just can't deal with that sort of thing.'
I felt it was best to change the subject.

'So what are you doing in Paris Lady Louise?' I asked.

'Oh please forget the 'Lady' bit, just call me Louise. Well I came for a break and to soak up some French culture. I've been very lucky in life, my father made an absolute fortune in industrial engineering, and being their only child my parents have always spoilt me rotten. I'm here on my own visiting art galleries, the ballet, I want to see an opera while I'm here, go to one or two classical concerts, holding afternoon tea parties etc, and then in a few weeks' time I'll return to the family estate in Berkshire.'

'I take it you're not married then?' asked Sam.

'No, I'm afraid not' she answered. 'I've never met the right man. I've had plenty of offers, and that's par for the course in the circles

my parents move in, but I felt they were all 'Hooray Henry' types. Look, I know' she continued starting to get excited 'why don't you two come to afternoon tea at my hotel tomorrow. I've get a few other guests coming, all English, and they'll be fascinated to hear about your adventures with Interpol.'
Before I could object or say anything Sam said

'That would be fabulous Louise, where and when?'

'I have a suite of rooms at the Four Seasons Hotel George V, three o'clock, and casual dress please, nothing too formal. Look I must go, but I'm so pleased to have met you both and I look forward to chatting some more tomorrow'.
We all shook hands again and then she walked out of the Louvre.

'God, of all the people to bump into' Gemma thought 'I had to pick two bloody Interpol officers. Mind you, they may be worth cultivating as they can keep me informed as to what progress the police are making.'
Once Gemma had returned to the hotel she made a note in her diary of the meeting at the Louvre with Michael and Sam and their names. She always made notes in her diary of

everything as and when she thought of things, and then brought it fully up to date at the end of each day. However, Gemma had an afternoon tea to organize for tomorrow, so she telephoned down to room service and asked for someone to come to her suite straight away to take full instructions for her precise requirements.

Detective Chief Inspector Claude Moreau of the Police Nationale was getting pressure applied to him from every direction. The 'Ministre de l'Intérieur' which is French for the 'Minister of the Interior', or what the English would call the 'Home Secretary' was not a happy man. He was the man responsible for all the major law enforcement forces in France including the French National Police, and the French Gendarmerie, and as such he was also the man getting all the blame. He now had eleven murders to solve, although he obviously knew the name of the murderer, and according to Mrs Borgert's letters published in Le Figaro, there would be many more to follow. He sat at his desk and once more went through the list in front of him.

It comprised of five pertinent questions: Who, When, How, Where and Why?

After 'Who' he had simply written 'Mrs Borgert'

with a note underneath asking 'Who the hell is she?' After the 'When' he had written the dates of the poisonings at the restaurant and the hospital. After the 'How' he had written Cyanide and Thallium. After the 'Where' he had written the locations of the restaurant and the hospital, and lastly under the 'Why' he had written Revenge, with a note underneath asking 'Revenge for what?'

There was a knock at his door. He said 'Entrer' and looked up to see his young assistant, Detective Inspector Hugo Duchand enter the room.

'Look, I don't know how you feel about this sir, but if you remember there were two Interpol officers at 'Cuisine Raffinée' when the seven poisonings occurred, and it occurs to me that one way of taking the pressure off you and this department is to ask for Interpol's help and put the pressure on them'.

'I don't know Hugo' replied his boss 'I hate asking for outside help. It feels like I'm saying we're incompetent and can't solve this thing ourselves.'

'Not being funny sir, but we haven't a clue who this Mrs Borgert is, why she's doing it, or where and when she's going to strike next. I don't think the Minister is going to sit on this for much longer without demanding your head on a plate, and most of us getting served up with it.'

'No, you're right there Hugo. He's a bloody politician and not a policeman'.

'The other thing is sir, this Mrs Borgert woman writes her letters in English. Now that could be because she's English or American or Australian or anywhere else they speak English, but wherever she comes from that makes it international, and therefore it makes sense to call in Interpol. I know you don't like doing it sir, but it might help you keep your job!'

'Yes, as usual you're right Hugo. Find out who I have to call to officially ask for their cooperation, I don't actually want to ask for their help as such.'

'Already done it sir, just in case you asked. It's Chief Superintendent Helena Van Houten, Interpol's Head of European Operations, here's her telephone number. Hugo handed a slip of paper to his boss who immediately picked up the phone on his desk and dialled.'

Chapter Twelve

I was having a cup of tea in our hotel room and Sam was in the shower when my mobile rang. I could see from the phone's display that it was Helena ringing from Interpol's Operations HQ in Amsterdam.

'Good morning young man' she began 'and how are you and your poor long suffering wife enjoying the delights of Paris?'

'Oh not so bad' I replied. 'We're off to have afternoon tea later today with a very nice English lady we met yesterday at the Canaletto exhibition in the Louvre, and then we thought we might try the Moulin Rouge this evening.'

'That sounds wonderful, and I don't want to rain on your parade, but I've just received a telephone call from a Detective Chief Inspector Claude Moreau who is heading up the search for the Paris Poisoner, and he has officially asked if Interpol can cooperate with the French police in trying to track down this mysterious Mrs Borgert. You and Sam are already on the spot so to speak, and so it makes sense if you are Interpol's initial response, plus you were there in the restaurant when it all kicked off. What do you think, can you help? Obviously it will be official and you'll get the usual remuneration and back up from head office etc'.

'I'll have to check with Sam, but I'm sure

she'll say yes. Assuming she does, how do you want us to handle this?'

'Well I noticed our Detective Chief Inspector didn't actually ask me for our help, just our cooperation, so I think this is more of a political move designed to protect his own backside. Be careful in your dealings with him, get what you can out of him and in return feed him the occasional tit bit, but if you happen to get a really good lead, deal with it yourself. If at any point in this you need back up, ask me not Detective Chief Inspector Moreau, and lastly as this is now an official Interpol enquiry you'll need to keep in touch at least every other day and let me know what's happening.'

'Thanks Helena, will do'.

'Enjoy your afternoon tea, and make sure the cakes haven't been poisoned'.

'You're such a cheerful soul aren't you?' I laughed 'Bye'.

I filled Sam in on our conversation as soon as she emerged from the shower, and as I thought she was very happy to get involved.

We arrived at the Four Seasons Hotel George V at the appointed hour, and walked over to the lady on the reception desk.

'Bonjour monsieur, bonjour Madame.

Comment puis-je vous aider?'

'Excusez-moi' I replied in my extremely poor French 'Parlez-vous Anglais?'

'Of course sir. The staff here at the reception desk of the Four Seasons speak twenty three languages between us, and English is one of the languages we are all required to speak. So, my name is Claudette and how can I help you sir?'

'Thank you Claudette' I answered 'we have an appointment for afternoon tea with Lady Louise Hamilton Smythe'.

'Of course sir, I'll just check my list. Your names please?'

'Michael and Samantha Turner' I replied.

'Thank you Mr Turner' Claudette replied ticking our names off on her list. 'You'll find Lady Hamilton Smythe and her other guests in her private suite. That's the Ambassador Suite on the fourth floor. The lift is over there to your left. Please, enjoy your tea.'

I thanked her and Sam and I wandered over to the lifts. Everything about the hotel oozed grand opulence. The floors were either magnificent Italian marble or glorious thick pile carpet, and everywhere you looked there were numerous luxurious sofas and armchairs, all surrounded by enough flowers to have emptied Kew

Gardens. Even the lifts felt grand. We arrived at the door of the Ambassador suite and rang the bell on the wall to the side. The door was opened by a liveried waiter who took our names and then announced us as we walked into the first room. Lady Louise cut short the conversation she was having and bounded over to us.

'Michael, Sam, I'm so pleased you could make it.' then very quietly she almost whispered 'I'm so glad you two are here, I can't stand the pompous lot that I'm currently talking to, but there aren't that many English people in Paris at the moment so you have to take pot luck. Come and join us.'

Lady Louise indicated to one of the waiters who brought over a tray of porcelain cups, saucers and a teapot along with a three tier cake tray containing beautifully cut sandwiches and a vast array of pastries. Milk, lemon and sugar was already on the table in front of us. We sat on the chairs indicated and Lady Louise introduced us to some of her other guests.

'These lovely people are Michael and Samantha Turner and they live in the Algarve in Portugal. I'll leave them to tell you exactly what they do. These are my good friends Sir Ralph and Lady Daphne Carmichael who are here on holiday from Dorset, and this handsome gentleman is the honourable Mr Douglas Philpott, the British Consul here in Paris.' Everyone offered everyone else good afternoons along with handshakes all round.

'So what do you and Michael do then Samantha?' asked Lady Carmichael. 'Louise made it sound as if you do something terribly exciting.'

'Oh, I don't know about that' said Sam smiling. 'I used to be a police surgeon in the UK, but I now run my own private medical practice in the Algarve. Michael used to write very successful crime thrillers, but he is now concentrating on travel guides, and when we're not doing either of those two things we both work as investigative consultants for Interpol.'

'See, I told you they'd be worth meeting' oozed Louise. 'I told everyone that I bumped into you two at the Louvre yesterday, and that I felt sure you'd be very interesting people to talk to. See, I was right.'

Lady Louise was almost childlike in her enthusiasm, but I put it down to the relief of not having to continue making conversation with her other guests, who from what I'd seen so far mostly seemed to be quite elderly and basically very dull.

'Tell me' said the British Consul 'are you

two involved in investigating these bloody awful poisonings going on?'

'As it happens' replied Sam 'the French police have just requested Interpol to assist them in their enquiries, and Michael and I are now officially on the case so to speak.'

'Yes' I jumped in 'We'd heard unsubstantiated rumours that Sir Ralph might be posing as this Mrs Borgert woman when you are asleep Lady Carmichael, and so we've come to afternoon tea in order to interrogate him.' Everyone laughed, including Sir Ralph. 'Please ignore my husband' said Sam 'he has a distinctly warped sense of humour'.

'No, please, you interrogate away old chap' Sir Ralph said smiling. 'You never know, I might learn something about myself. Perhaps I go sleepwalking during the night and poison anyone I see before returning to bed?'

'Ah, well that's it then' I declared 'case solved. Sam, get your handcuffs out.'

'Seriously' said Douglas Philpott 'this is a very worrying situation, and I as British Consul have to advise anyone from the UK visiting Paris as to whether they should stay and carry on as normal, or leave. What would your advice be?'

'To be honest Douglas' I replied 'we were only asked to get involved two hours ago, and at this stage you probably know as much about it as we do.'

'If it was me' said Sam thoughtfully 'I'd just leave and come back to Paris when all this is over, but as I say, that's just me personally. Safety first and all that.'

We continued talking, drinking tea and eating cakes for another two hours and we all left around five o'clock. We decided to keep our thoughts to ourselves regarding the poisonings and share nothing of what we knew or what conclusions we had come to, after all we had no real idea who any of these people were. Douglas, the British Consul seemed a nice enough man and Sir Ralph and Lady Carmichael were pleasant enough although their conversation was fairly limited to countryside pursuits and their home in Dorset. There were half a dozen other guests we'd met but in all honesty none of them made a lasting impression. Then there was our host, Lady Louise Hamilton Smythe. She made quite an impact on us both. Me, because I thought she was incredibly attractive with a great figure and a lovely personality, and Sam who thought she was too rich and far too attractive to still be single, so there must be something wrong with her that we were unaware of.

Chapter Thirteen

Once all the guests had gone Lady Louise changed out of her fine maroon dress and gold jewellery, she had a long hot soak in the bath, grabbed a few hours' sleep and woke up when the alarm she'd set earlier went off at 10.30 pm. Lady Louise got dressed into smart, but quite casual clothes and immediately she put them on she started thinking and behaving like Mrs Gemma Borgert. It was uncanny and she was totally aware of it herself, and she felt as Gemma she could be her true self. So far her campaign had been successful, but she was also aware that the longer this went on the more likely she was to get caught. She'd slipped on a smart lightweight camel coloured suede zip fronted jacket over her designer jeans and white polo neck top and now dressed she headed out of the hotel. Gemma's destination was number 71 Rue Albert, 75013 Paris, which just happened to be the principal building in Paris of the 'Préfecture de Police', or in simple English, the Police headquarters. Tonight was just recognisance. She needed to watch certain people coming and going from the Préfecture de Police HQ, and she knew that particular activity would all happen around midnight. Gemma arrived in Rue Albert at 11.45 pm and sat at an outside table of a coffee bar that was still open. She ordered a white coffee and a pastry and sat watching the main entrance. By 12.20 am Gemma had seen more than enough, she paid her bill leaving a nice tip and made her way back to the Four Seasons.

The following morning, I telephoned Chief Inspector Claude Moreau, introduced myself and asked if Sam and I could meet with him later that day. He readily agreed and suggested 11.00 am in his office. We duly arrived on time and were met in reception by his assistant, Detective Inspector Hugo Duchand.

'Good morning Mr and Mrs Turner' he said in a friendly voice. 'Welcome to the headquarters of the Police Nationale. I have to say it's very unusual to find a husband and wife team working together in this line of business'.

'Ah well' said Sam 'I had to you see, mixing with all these criminals I have to ensure Michael always stays on the straight and narrow.'

'I'm sorry' Hugo replied. 'The straight and narrow what? I speak reasonably good English I think, but I do not understand all the little sayings you have.'

'Ignore my wife Hugo' I jumped in smiling. 'I try to do so as much as I can. Sorry dear, you know I'm only joking.'

'I'm afraid it's the English sense of humour' said Sam 'and I'm now thinking you have to be English to fully appreciate it.'

'I see, I think' said Hugo smiling. He knocked on the door of Chief Inspector Claude Moreau's office and upon receiving an 'Entrer' he opened the door and we all walked in. Claude Moreau was a large well-built man, perhaps a little too round at his waist, aged I would guess around 60. He had a large moustache, but was most decidedly going thin on top. He came forward and shook hands with both of us.

'Good morning Mr and Mrs Turner and welcome, please may I ask, do you speak French or would you prefer we converse in English?'

'English would be better if that is OK with you Chief Inspector' said Sam 'and please call us Sam and Michael.'

'In that case you must call me Claude and my colleague here is Hugo.'

'Thank you Claude' I said.

'Now I spoke on the telephone with your Chief Superintendent Helena van Houten and due to the possible international aspect of this Mrs Borgert affair, I felt it was best if the Police National and Interpol collaborated. She informed me that the two of you were already here in Paris, which I already knew from our own report on the mass poisonings at the restaurant, and she felt it would be best if the four of us worked together if that is alright with you both?'

'Sounds fine and makes a lot of sense' I responded.

'Excellent' said Claude. 'Now I gather from your Chief Superintendent that you worked out what poison had been used and how it had been administered while you were both still at the restaurant, but you did not forward that information on to us at the Police National. Any reason why not?' he asked.

'Sorry Claude' I said 'but we weren't 100% sure, we were just making guesses from what we had seen. Sam used to be a police surgeon and is very familiar with death by various poisons, and she felt the only poison that worked that fast was cyanide, but it was only a guess. Likewise, I walked around the restaurant examining all the plates of those that had died and as far as I could tell the only food they all had in common was raw tomato, but again, it was just a guess, and not a fact. By the time we woke up the following morning the whole of Paris knew it was cyanide poison injected into the tomatoes thanks to Mrs Borgert's letter in Le Figaro.'

'I see, well that's fair enough' responded Claude 'and I thank you for your honesty. I also gather the two of you were here in Paris last year and were involved in that dreadful fracas with the terrorists?'

'Yes we were' said Sam. 'Your President Cazeneuve very kindly booked us into the Hotel de Marigny as his personal guests, and we had several pleasant meetings with him, even though we were dealing with very serious matters. Gilles has a great sense of humour and we always get on famously'

I knew immediately what Sam was doing, she was making sure Claude knew we had contacts and influence at the highest possible level here in France, so in the nicest possible way she was saying, don't mess with us.

'I'm afraid I've never had the opportunity of meeting him myself, but he seems to be doing a good job.'

'Is there anything you need us to do as outsiders that is difficult for you to do as the French police? You mentioned to Helena the possible international aspect of this case, may I ask, what exactly are you referring to Claude?'

'Well the fact that she writes her letters to Le Figaro in English. That could indicate she is English, or American, Australian etc, or she could still be French and just be trying to 'put us off the scent' as you English say. We have checked all the Mrs Borgert's we have listed here in France and nobody stands out as being in the least bit suspicious, but Interpol have access to all the Borgert's world-wide.'

'Helena's already done that' said Sam 'no joy I'm afraid.'

'Yes' I added 'Helena went through all the Borgert's on Interpol's date base, but like you nobody stood out as being a possible suspect.'

'If you don't mind me asking' said Claude 'I and all my officers always refer to senior officers by their title, and yet you both refer to Chief Superintendent van Houten as Helena. Is that level of informality normal within Interpol?'

'No it's not' answered Sam. 'We originally called her by her title, but over the years we've become such good friends that Helena was my chief bridesmaid at our wedding. I think I can honestly say she really is my best friend.'

'Mm, President's, the head of Interpol,

anyone else I should know about so that I don't put my foot in it?' asked Claude with a smile.

'Well we know the UK Prime Minister, the Foreign Secretary and the Home Secretary very well, along with the President of the United States and the Chancellor of Germany. We're also on first name terms with the head of operations at MI6 and the head of Mossad, who incidentally is a really nice man.'

'I think I'm going to have to watch my step with you two aren't I?' said Claude. 'One step out of place and you'll have me done away with.'

'Oh come on Claude' smiled Sam 'we may know all these people, but it's all been through work. Forget about it and let's all get on with finding the wretched Mrs Borgert.'

Chapter Fourteen

At just before 10.30 pm, Gemma left her hotel and headed off to the grotty single room apartment she'd rented in the side street near Le Figaro's offices. She put her own smart but casual clothes in the wardrobe and dressed herself in the old the flowery dress and shoes she'd worn last time she was there. To this she added the grey wig ensuring her own dark hair was well hidden, and a set of brown overalls she'd bought earlier in the day at a local hardware store. While at the hardware shop she'd also bought a grey plastic bucket, a wooden scrubbing brush, a bottle of bleach based cleaning fluid and several yellow dusters. Her other purchase that day had been at the opticians, a pair of virtually clear glass silver rimmed reading glasses. She had deliberately 'dirtied' the overalls and scrunched them up so that they didn't look new, and to finish off the image she put on the spectacles and tied an old dark green headscarf around the wig.

She then put a blue plastic lunchbox in the bottom of the bucket that contained a couple of cheese sandwiches. However, inside the sandwiches she had secreted two syringes of thallium, the last of her supplies. On top of the two sandwiches she dropped in an apple and a bag of crisps. Checking in the mirror on the front of the wardrobe door she decided she would have to do, and headed off to her destination - 71 Rue Albert, 75013 Paris, the principal building of the 'Préfecture de Police' - Police HQ.

The previous night she had stood opposite the building and watched all the cleaners coming and going. What she was about to do was risky as for a start, her French was virtually non-existent, but it was an extremely large building and she estimated there must be at least forty cleaners. Once inside and past reception she would be free to wander to her hearts content, and she decided the best approach was to latch on to a bunch of cleaners going in. As far as she'd seen the night before, nobody had to use a pass or show ID, so it shouldn't be too difficult. The cleaners started arriving about 11.50 pm, and they all simply waved at the officer on the reception desk before spreading out around the building. Gemma waited until she saw a few arriving together, and seeing the desk officer was busy dealing with a member of the public Gemma quickly attached herself to the back of the group of cleaners. The cleaners all looked and dressed more or less the same, a group of middle aged women, in dark blue or brown overalls, and all carrying buckets full of brushes and dusters. They all walked through the front door, waved at the officer on the reception desk and once inside they all dispersed in different directions. Gemma quickly broke away from the group she'd walked in with and headed upstairs. She hadn't a clue where she was going, but felt sure she would find an opportunity to do her worst somewhere in the building. There was nothing apart from offices on the first floor, and the second floor was no better, but she found exactly what she was looking for on the third floor - the staff canteen. Gemma needed to avoid the other cleaners as much as possible, but unfortunately there were two cleaners already in the canteen. Gemma locked herself in the nearest ladies toilet she could find and decided to wait thirty minutes before checking again. When she did return to the canteen she was just in time to see the two cleaners she'd spotted earlier leaving, deep in conversation. Nobody was in sight, and as far as Gemma could tell, nobody knew she was even in the building.

Gemma entered the canteen but all left the lights off. There were glass panels in the double doors and she didn't want to risk being seen. There was enough ambient light coming in for her see more or less what she was doing. She went straight to the two fridges behind the serving counter and opened the first. It contained amongst other food items a large joint of cold ham which had already been partially sliced, and Gemma took out her first syringe of thallium and injected a small into two different areas of the ham. There were also about ten large bottles of milk in the first fridge. Unscrewing the lids of three of them, she injected the remains of her first syringe into those three bottles. Gemma then ensured the three were positioned at the front of the shelf making sure they would get used first. Inside the second fridge she found various packets of different kinds of processed food, but nothing that screamed out 'inject me' to her. Anyway, the first syringe was now completely empty, so taking the second one out of her lunch box she injected small amounts of thallium into the various items of fresh fruit she saw sitting in a large wicker basket on the serving counter. In total she had enough to inject six oranges, four apples and two bananas. Her work now complete and with both syringes empty, she returned the syringes to her lunch box which she put in the bottom of her bucket. She piled the brush and the dusters on top, left the canteen and checking everywhere she went Gemma slowly made her way down the stairs and headed back towards reception. The last thing she needed now was to get caught, so she waited behind a column for about ten minutes until she saw a group of three cleaners about to leave. As they started walking past the reception desk Gemma tagged along about three or four feet behind them searching through her bucket as she left to avoid any eye contact. The officer on the desk looked up, but barely acknowledged their existence. They all walked out of the building and a very relieved Gemma slowly made her way back to the apartment. Once inside her room she got changed back into her normal clothes, and after another leisurely walk to help her calm down, she was back inside the Four Seasons by 2.00 am.

24 hours later Gemma delivered her third letter to Oscar Dubois. She'd sat at her laptop and carefully composed the letter to the editor of Le Figaro. She wrote several versions and in the end rejected them all. If she wasn't careful she was going to give the game away by saying too much in her letters, so in the end she kept it very simple.

Monsieur Oscar Dubois
Editor
Le Figaro

To the people of Paris

I have been busy again, and this time I have had my revenge on various members of the police force of this city. When I needed them they let me down, so it is now their turn to die. Again, I have no idea how

many have died or will die, and I really do not care, the more the merrier!
Beware people of Paris - I have still not finished.

Mrs Borgert

It was 9.00 am when the third letter arrived on Oscar Dubois' desk. Le Figaro had now installed a uniformed security man near reception whose job was to stop and interrogate anyone delivering a single letter to the editor. But Gemma had seen this new addition and so she decided against dropping any future letters on the desk of reception, and instead she would adopt a new strategy. At 7.30 am he following morning, dressed in her elderly lady outfit, she dropped her letter into Le Figaro's post box on the outside of the building. She had deliberately avoided using this post box previously as there was a CCTV camera positioned about fifteen feet up the wall directly above the post box, but she decided dressed as she was and providing she kept her head down she should be fine even if they did see her on CCTV. Unbeknown to Gemma at this stage and in the thirty two hours since she'd walked out of the police HQ dressed as a cleaner, six police officers had now died from thallium poisoning. Chief Inspector Claude

Moreau upon hearing of the first death had immediately ordered that no more food or drinks were to be consumed in police HQ and because of his swift action, there were only the six fatalities. But that was still six too many.

Chapter Fifteen

'OK Pierre' said Oscar. 'I've got another letter from Mrs Borgert.'

'What's she saying this time' he asked?

'Surprisingly little actually' replied Oscar. 'She just claims responsibility for killing the police officers and warns the people of Paris that she still hasn't finished.'

'By my reckoning' said Pierre 'that's seven dead at the restaurant, four doctors murdered and now six police officers killed. Seventeen perfectly innocent people dead, and all for some unknown reason. That must make her Paris's biggest ever serial killer doesn't it?'

'I don't know' replied Oscar. 'Check it out on the internet, it will probably tell us who was the biggest if it's not her.'

Pierre searched the internet and then read aloud from his screen.

'According to the internet, the biggest serial killer was Marcel Petiot who was a French doctor. He was convicted of multiple murders after the discovery of the remains of 23 people in the basement of his Paris home during World War Two. Good God Oscar, it says here that he is suspected of the murder of around 60 victims during his lifetime, although the true number remains unknown. Apart from him, it doesn't look like anyone else comes close to Mrs Borgert's tally of seventeen, with probably a damn site more to follow.'

OK' mused Oscar 'So we can legitimately describe Mrs Borgert as 'France's biggest serial killer since the Second World War.''

'Sounds good Oscar. I'll start working on it. Have you notified our beloved Chief Inspector Moreau about the arrival of her third letter yet?'

'Yes, he'll be here in about twenty minutes, and I gather he's bringing a couple of Interpol officers with him.'

Sam and I were woken up by the telephone at 9.10 am. We'd had a late night having had a very pleasant meal and a bottle of excellent Merlot in the hotel's restaurant, and then we both fell asleep on the sofa watching 'Casablanca' the late night movie on the TV in our bedroom.
The telephone call was from Chief Inspector

Moreau who informed us he was on his way to Le Figaro's offices as another letter had arrived from Mrs Borgert, and he wondered if we'd like to join him there at 9.45 if we could make it in time. Obviously we jumped at the chance, quickly threw some clothes on and jumped into a taxi. We made it with about three minutes to spare.

'Thanks for coming' Claude said. 'We've asked for your cooperation and you may well think of something we don't. I'll be honest Michael, mostly we don't like outside interference in our cases, but on this occasion I'll take all the help I can.'

'Don't worry Claude' I replied. 'It's the same with every police force we've worked with the world over.'

'Nobody likes calling in Interpol' said Sam 'as it always seems like you're saying we can't do this on our own.'

'Exactly' he said.

'But that's really not the case is it?' I said 'It's simply that because Interpol is truly international, we have access to numerous different resources not available to you, and in fact more resources than any individual countries internal police force.'

'I guess so' pondered Claude. 'Anyway,

we better go and see Oscar Dubois, the Editor of Le Figaro.'

Detective Inspector Hugo Duchand was with the chief Inspector and the four of us made our way the stairs to the first floor newsroom and editorial offices of France's largest daily newspaper. We walked past what seemed like hundreds of desks with people typing madly into their computers, and eventually we reached a quiet office at the far end of the room. Claude knocked on the door, received an 'Entrer' and the four of us entered the room. As well as the Editor Oscar Dubois, his News Editor Pierre Faucheux was also in the room. Pierre walked over to the door and closed it while Claude did all the introductions.

'OK Oscar' said Claude 'What's she got to say for herself this time?'

'Not a great deal I'm afraid. Just that she has killed an unknown number of police officers and that she hasn't finished.'

Oscar pressed a button on his computer keyboard and Mrs Borgert's letter appeared on the large TV monitor opposite Oscar's desk. We all read it in silence.

'That settles it' I said 'Mrs Borgert is definitely English'.

'How the hell do you know that' asked

Pierre?

'Because' said Sam who had spotted the same thing as me 'only a true English man or English woman would say 'The more the merrier.'

'It's an old English expression dating from around the time of King James the first.' I said 'Basically it means something is always better with more people involved, or in Mrs Borgert's warped mind, more dead bodies.'

'I agree' said Sam 'Mrs Borgert has to be English, or at least born and brought up there.'

'But Borgert is not an English name is it?' queried Oscar.

'No, but then Borgert is her married name isn't it' answered Sam. 'She could have been born with a very boring English name like plain old Mrs Smith, Mrs Brown or Mrs Jones.'

'I hate to be pedantic dear' I cut in 'but Jones is a Welsh name, not English.'

'Don't lie Michael' Sam came back at me. 'You love being pedantic, you revel in being pedantic, your entire life is built around being bloody pedantic.'
I could see everyone else was looking uncomfortable, and they were staring at us.

'But despite your incredibly annoying and usually totally pointless pedantic predilections' Sam said smiling 'I still for some unearthly reason love you to bits.' at which point Sam leant in and kissed me on the cheek.

'Thank you dear' I smiled 'I love you too'. Everyone laughed and Claude said.

'Thank god for that. Can we move on please folks?'

'The problem is' said Oscar 'we still don't know what this is all about. She's now murdered seventeen people in revenge. But revenge for what?'

'So ask her' I said.

'What do you mean' queried Oscar.

'Look' I replied 'she writes to you using Le Figaro, so write back to her in Le Figaro asking various questions. Why are you doing this, revenge for what, when will all this be over etc? She probably won't answer any of your questions, but she may accidentally drop a few clues.'

'That's an excellent idea Michael' enthused Claude. 'We should make out a list of questions.'

'Yes' I agreed 'but don't overdo it, at least not to start with. One very simple question like 'Revenge for what?' may get a reply. We can go ask more in future editions. After all Le Figaro is a daily newspaper, so let's ask a question a day.'

'I like it' said Oscar. 'So tomorrow's edition should ask 'Revenge for what?'

'Yes, I think so' I said. 'It may make her open up a bit and in doing so give us the odd clue or two. Let's be honest here, as Oscar said earlier, she's now murdered seventeen innocent people and we don't know why she's doing it, who she is, where to find her, we are still as much in the dark as when this whole damn thing started.'

'No, we do know she's English however, or at least we think she is' said Sam. 'I guess you and I could always go to England tomorrow and search the marriage records at the General Register Office in Southport and see if there is a record of an English woman marrying a Mr Borgert? We've been there twice before re other cases and they're pretty helpful.'

'That's true' I replied 'I don't think there's much we can do here Claude, so why don't Sam and I see if we can get a lead in the UK. It may well come to nothing, but it's got to be worth a try.'

'I agree. Oscar will ask her about revenge for what in tomorrow's newspaper and I suspect it will be another day before we get an answer, by which time you may both be back.'

'I've just looked online' said Pierre 'and

the nearest full international airport to Southport is Manchester, and there is a flight from Charles de Gaulle at 6.00 pm this evening. Do you want me to book you a couple of tickets?'

'Please Pierre' said Sam.

'OK' I said 'In that case we'll love you and leave you and head back to our hotel. If we arrive in Manchester tonight we should find what we want, if there is anything to find tomorrow, and then be back here in Paris the day after, by when we'll have hopefully heard back from Mrs Borgert.'

Chapter Sixteen

We arrived at Manchester airport around 9.00 pm and checked into one of the many hotels that surround the airport. The following morning we showered, had a decent breakfast, picked up a hire car and headed for the General Register Office.

The General Register Office came into being in 1836 was originally based in the North wing of Somerset House in London, where it remained until 1970 when it moved to St Catherine's House on Kingsway, also in London. However, in 1997 the GRO staff were all moved to Southport, Merseyside while public access to the records and indexes was made available at a new Family Records Centre in south London. The Family Records Centre was eventually closed to the public in 2008, due to decreasing visitor numbers caused by the online availability of the records.

Sam and I arrived at the offices having made a telephone appointment with the manager, a Mrs Gwenda Cartwright, who made us very welcome.

'I do believe you are the first Interpol officers I have ever met' said Mrs Cartwright having carefully examined our Interpol warrant cards.

'We have actually been here once before' said Sam 'during another case, but we dealt with one of your colleagues, a Mr Peterson if I remember rightly.'

'Ah, yes, Sam Peterson' she mused. 'A lovely man, he now works at the DVLA offices in Swansea I believe. Anyway, how can I help you now you are here? You said on the telephone that you were looking for a marriage between an unknown English woman and a man named Mr Borgert. Christian name and nationality unknown, and marriage date unknown. Is that correct?'

'Yes, it is' I answered. 'I know it's a pretty forlorn hope but it is important.'

'Would I be right' asked Mrs Cartwright 'in assuming it's to do with all those poisonings in Paris? It's been in all the newspapers and on the television?'

'Yes, you are quite right' replied Sam. 'We have both been assigned to the case, and we believe there's a good chance that this Mrs Borgert may be English. We may well be wrong, but we wanted to rule it out if we are wrong.'

'Well I don't know if this is any help to you, but as you may or may not know, Church of England Ministers are also birth, deaths and marriage registrars, and one of their duties is that every vicar or rector in England is required to send us a list of all the births, deaths and marriages in their church every three months.'

'Please tell me you have a marriage record for a Mr and Mrs Borgert?' I excitedly asked.

'As it happens, we do' she smiled. 'A three month record list came in from a small country parish in Worcestershire last week listing the marriage of a Miss Gemma Louise Smith to a Mr Matthias Borgert. The wedding was just over four months ago. I'm afraid I have no more details available at this stage other than that which I've told you, but the vicar of the parish, a Revd. Arthur P. Featherstone may be able to help you further. I have printed you a copy of the marriage certificate, and this is the address of the church and vicarage.'

'Mrs Cartwright, I could happily kiss you' I enthused.

'Well don't let me stop you dear' laughed Sam. So I did. I leant in and before she could stop me I kissed Mrs Cartwright on the cheek.

'Please forgive my husband' said Sam laughing 'and yes, we are happily married, but he loves his work, and you could have just helped crack this case.'

'It has been my pleasure' beamed Mrs Cartwright, whose face had now turned a shade of blush pink.

We left the offices and sat outside in our hire car.

'What now' I asked Sam. 'Do we go straight to Worcestershire or fly back to Paris with what we know?'

'I think we have to drive to Worcestershire and see this vicar. He may be able to remember the wedding and give us some more useful information.'

'What do you reckon, fly to Worcester, train or drive? I asked.

'Oh let's just drive. By the time we've

returned the car, caught a train, picked up another hire car etc, we can probably be there.'
So we set off for the Worcestershire countryside.

The Revd. Arthur P. Featherstone was fast asleep in the back garden of the vicarage, when we arrived having his usual afternoon siesta. His wife Molly, was busy baking bread in the kitchen. She welcomed us into the vicarage, requested we sit down in the small, but pleasant lounge and then she went outside to get her husband.

Revd. Featherstone was a small man and I estimated from his appearance that he was well past retirement age, but like a lot of Church of England clergymen, they were never forced to retire by their respective Bishop if they didn't want to. The main reason these days seemed to be lack of recruitment and therefore very little new blood in the form of eager young curates coming into the system.

'Good morning' said the vicar entering the room 'Mr and Mrs Turner I believe my wife said. How can I help you?'
He sat down in an armchair, and after we took out our Interpol badges and warrants and showed them to him, we sat opposite him and his wife on the sofa.

'We are very interested in a couple you married about four months ago' said Sam 'and we wondered what you could tell us about them?'

'And what couple might that be?' he asked.

'A Mr and Mrs Borgert' I replied.

'Ah yes' he said slowly thinking back 'A German gentleman if I remember rightly, and a pretty dark haired English lady. I remember them both very well. Being a small parish in the middle of the countryside, we do not get very many weddings. In fact we get very little of anything in this parish. Very few births, a few deaths here and there, and with a congregation of just fourteen regulars, very little gossip' he said laughing at his own joke.

'What can you tell us about Mr and Mrs Borgert?' I asked again.

'Mm, let me think' he said. 'Well, as I said before, he was a German gentleman, but he spoke excellent English. A doctor of some sort I believe.
I don't know what she did for a living, if anything, but she was certainly very bright.'

'Did they mention their plans to you at all?' asked Sam.

'No, not really. All they said was that

after their honeymoon they hoped to settle down in the countryside somewhere, but with easy access to London so that Mr Borgert could work.'

'No more than that?' I asked.

'No' he simply replied. 'They didn't want to talk, they just wanted to get married. They got two people passing by the church to act as their witnesses and they were in and out within fifteen minutes. No organ or choir, no white dress, no bridesmaids, no best man, it was all very quick. They thanked me and rushed off in their car.'

'Can you tell us anything about the car?' Sam asked.

'It was dark blue, but beyond that I have no idea. I don't drive and I know nothing about cars I'm afraid.'

Sam and I looked at each other, and realized there was nothing more to be gained by staying any longer, so we thanked the vicar and his wife for their hospitality and got up to leave. The vicar and his wife came out to wave us off, and as we were about to get into our hire car Sam suddenly turned round and said

'I don't suppose either of them happened to mention where they were going for their honeymoon?'

'Yes' replied Mrs Fairbrother. 'Paris'.
We looked at each other, smiled, got in the car and headed for the airport.

Chapter Seventeen.

We got back to our hotel later that night having caught the first flight back to Paris, and we collapsed into bed completely exhausted, but we felt we'd made pretty good progress. We couldn't be one hundred percent sure, but we were ninety nine percent sure Mrs Borgert was the English wife of a German doctor named Matthias Borgert.
It didn't solve the case, far from it, but at least we had a few more clues to go on.

'Michael' said Sam in the dark, both lying awake in bed.

'Can't you sleep either?' I asked.

'I was just wondering' answered Sam 'how much of what we've found out we share with Claude and the French police. Don't get me wrong, I like Claude, but ideally I'd like time to think it all through for ourselves before we say anything.'

'I agree completely. We haven't really had time to collect our thoughts, and I'd like to take our time before saying anything. However, we do have to meet up with Claude later today, and we have to say something.'

'We can always say it was a dead end' said Sam 'but they'll let us know if anything comes to light. After all, nobody except you and me know exactly what was said and what it means.'

'I know what was said' I replied 'but without time to think it all through I'm not sure what it actually means. Perhaps this is the break we've been waiting for, or on the other hand it may turn out to mean absolutely nothing.'

'So are we agreed?' asked Sam 'we tell Claude we learnt nothing of any use from the records department in England, but they will keep searching and let us know the minute they find anything useful.'

'Deal' I replied, and within three minutes we were both asleep.

Lady Louise was awake bright and early and decided she needed to top up the culture level in her life during the next couple of days. She'd done the ballet and she'd done the Louvre, so what was left. Theatre was out as all the plays were in French, so that left either an opera or a classical music concert. Being a single woman in Paris and in particular attending the right sort of functions as a single woman was difficult on her own, she definitely needed companions. I know she thought, I'll ask Michael and Sam to come with me and they can choose. They may be Gemma's enemy, but they are my friends. Then she thought about what she had just thought to herself. Not only was she dressing and acting like two different people, she was actually thinking of Gemma and Lady Louise as being two different people.

She picked up her mobile and dialled Michael's number. It was ringing.

'Michael Turner' I said in a weary voice.

'Sorry Michael, it's Lady Louise, have I woken you up and if so I'm sorry?'

'Yes, but please don't worry about it. What can we do for you?'

'I need a culture fix this evening, and I'd like you two join me as my guests.'

'What exactly did you have in mind?' I asked.

'Either an opera or a classical music concert - you choose.

'Oh, a classical concert is far more my cup of tea' I replied.

'Excellent, I'll leave that with you then. You choose, book three tickets and I'll reimburse you when we meet up for drinks before the concert. Bye Michael.'

The phone went dead and I collapsed back onto my pillow.

'Who was that and what the hell do they want at this unearthly hour of the morning' asked Sam? By the way, what time is it?'

I looked at the bedside clock.

'Hell, it's nearly 8.30.' I cursed 'We're due to meet Claude at Le Figaro at 9.30. We better get moving. You can have the shower first.'

'Thanks' said Sam moving towards the bathroom 'but you still haven't said who that was on the phone.'

'Oh, it was Louise' I replied. 'I think I agreed we'd go with her to either a concert or the opera tonight. She left it to me to choose.'

'I thought you couldn't stand opera?' said a voice fighting with the noise of the shower.

'I can't stand it' I answered. 'I have to say I'm not particularly fanatical about spending half of my annual income on a vastly overpriced ticket to listen to a vastly overweight battleship of a woman wearing a vastly oversized marquee shaped nightdress masquerading as an evening gown topped with a Viking helmet, burst my poor delicate eardrums by screaming in agony as loud and as high as possible and then having the bloody nerve to call it singing.'

'You're not keen then' laughed Sam.

'You could say that' I replied laughing myself. 'When we've finished with Claude I'll nip over to the Four Seasons and get the concierge to book three tickets for a classical concert and I'll ask him to charge it directly to Louise's account. He knows us well enough by now, and Louise won't mind.'

We had our meeting with Claude, Hugo, Oscar and Pierre at Le Figaro and told them what Sam and I had agreed earlier. Oscar had not had a reply to his letter on the front page of today's paper yet, but he said he would call us all the minute he heard anything. Having left Le Figaro's offices we made our way over to the Four Seasons. The concierge as I'd said knew us both and was happy to help. There were three concerts on that evening. A 'Wagner Evening' with selections from his famous 'Ring Cycle', a bit too heavy for my liking. 'An Encounter with Beethoven' which sounded better until I read through the programme. I was hoping for excerpts from the 'Fifth symphony' and the 'Choral movement from the Ninth', but no, this again was a really heavy programme of his lesser known works. However, the third concert was absolutely perfect for me being advertised as 'Selections from the Very Best of Classical Music.' Programme selection is always a matter of taste, but whoever chose these was on my wavelength. Rachmaninov's 'Rhapsody on a theme of Paganini', Elgar's 'Nimrod' from the 'Enigma variations', Gustav Holst's 'Mars' from 'The Planets', Rossini's 'The Thieving Magpie', Mascagni's 'Intermezzo' from 'Cavalleria Rusticana' and finishing with the final movement of Stravinsky's magnificent 'Firebird Suite'. What was going to make the evening even better was that the concert was being given by the 'Orchestre de Paris' in the sensational new concert hall 'The Philharmonie de Paris'. We were in for a great evening in great company. Louise was always good fun and we both liked her a lot. Naturally, the concierge had checked with her before booking the tickets, but true to her word she said 'Whatever Michael has chosen is fine by me.'

In her suite, Lady Louise was busy getting changed into another of her smart casual outfits. This time smart black trousers with a white polo neck sweater, and on top, a casual maroon suede zip fronted jackets. She had four of these jackets, all different colours to suit her mood, and she felt the style suited her. Now dressed as she was, she felt she was now Gemma, and not Lady Louise. Earlier in the day, she'd got out the death certificate the doctor had written out when Matthias died, and she'd desperately been trying to trace him since then. The death certificate had been signed Dr Gaspard Boucher, but as far as she could tell he had either stopped practising medicine, had retired or had died. She really hoped it wasn't the latter as she hoped to do that particular deed for him.

Looking again at Matthias's death certificate she saw for the first time that there was an address she hadn't noticed before printed in very small letters underneath his name. It was 57 Rue Saint-Jacques. She had found it on a map of Paris and was off on a recognisance mission. She knew she'd recognize the doctor if she ever saw him again, and depending on what she found when she got, that would in her mind determine exactly how he was going to die although she already knew which poison she would use. Gemma had been buying poisons again from the same mail order supplier in Bulgaria, who seemed to be able to supply anything even though what she wanted had been banned from sale in the UK since 2006.

This time Gemma had purchased strychnine, not

thallium. Along with the poison she had also ordered a dozen syringes, and as she'd now decided to target specific individuals, she would need a comprehensive supply. In Gemma's mind and using her own logic, because Dr Gaspard Boucher had taken so long to arrive that fateful evening, poor Matthias had been in absolute agony for well over an hour before he died, and Gemma now wanted Dr Boucher to experience at least the same level of excruciating pain as her beloved husband had had to endure, and the best poison to use to achieve that aim was strychnine.

Gemma knew the symptoms of strychnine poisoning well from her medical training days at Oxford University. Ten to twenty minutes after exposure to the strychnine, the body's muscles would begin to spasm, starting with the head and neck in the form of 'trismus', which is basically a spasm of the jaw muscles, causing the mouth to remain tightly closed. This is followed by 'risus sardonicus', sometimes called a rictus grin where highly characteristic and abnormal spasms of the facial muscles cause an unearthly type of grin. The spasms then slowly spread to every muscle in the body, with nearly continuous convulsions, getting worse and worse at even the slightest stimulus. The convulsions progress, increasing in intensity and frequency until the backbone arches continually. These convulsions lead to 'lactic acidosis', which in layman's English means acute muscle cramps and pain, with severe abdominal pain. 'Rhabdomyolysis' follows which is basically the fast degeneration and then total destruction of all skeletal muscle tissue. Death usually comes from asphyxiation caused by paralysis roughly two hours after the initial exposure.

This then was Gemma's plan for Dr Gaspard Boucher.

Chapter Eighteen.

The concert had been absolutely fantastic, all my favourite pieces of classical music, while I was seated between two beautiful and very elegant ladies. What more could any man ask for? Being a classical concert performed in one of the smartest venues in the whole of Paris I was under strict instructions from Sam to 'dress to impress' which meant wearing a dinner jacket. I hired one for the evening from Louise's hotel and as I said, I couldn't have wished to have two more attractive and elegant ladies on my arms.

We met in the bar of the Four Seasons an hour or so before we were due to leave, and Louise had already phoned down and ordered a decent bottle of champagne to be put on ice with her name on it. We drank and chatted, and I have to say, conversation was easy and very relaxed, Louise was as usual really good company.

'Tell me you two' she said at one point 'how are you getting on with working with the French police and solving these wretched poisonings, have you cracked the case wide open yet?'

Sam and I had agreed we wouldn't talk about anything to do with the case with anyone, including Louise, and so we played dumb.

'Not really' I said dejectedly. 'As you know we briefly popped over to the UK to follow a potential lead, but it came to nothing, so we flew back here.'

'Surely the police must have some ideas?' Louise queried.

'Again, not really' said Sam. 'The problem is nobody has a clue why this Mrs Borgert woman is doing all this. She talks about getting her revenge, but revenge for what? Nobody has a clue what has upset her so much that she feels the need to turn into Frances biggest post war serial killer.'

'It's difficult' I said 'because we have no idea why she's doing this. With a motive you usually get a few clues, but at the moment Mrs Borgert could be anybody, and bear in mind, just because the letters are signed Mrs Borgert it doesn't necessarily mean it's a woman doing these killings, it could just as easily be a man trying to throw us off the scent.'

'Mm' Louise muttered. 'Well I don't envy you both. It sounds to me like this Mrs Borgert whoever he or she is, is running rings round the police and everybody else involved. No offence intended, but that includes you two as well.'

'No offence taken' said Sam. 'You're right, nobody has a clue who she is.'
Louise knew who Mrs Borgert was, but she said nothing and just smiled to herself.

Once she got back to her hotel suite after the concert Louise sat and thought back to the conversation she'd had earlier with Michael and Sam, and she decided not only did nobody know why people were dying, they had no idea what her poor husband had gone through. She picked up that morning's Le Figaro from the coffee table and looked at the front page again. The headline simply asked 'Vengeance pour quoi?' or in English 'Revenge for what?'

She decided it was about time that she answered their question.

The following morning, a plain white envelope appeared on Oscar's desk along with all the other post. It had no stamp, and it simply said 'OSCAR' in red ink on the envelope.

'How the hell did this arrive on my desk?' he asked nobody in particular.

'I guess someone must have dropped it on your desk as they walked past' replied Pierre. 'Why, what is it?'

'Looking at the writing on the envelope, which is in blood red ink, I am assuming it is from Mrs Borgert.'

'Well stop talking and open the bloody envelope Oscar.' said Pierre.

Oscar did as he was asked and pulled out the letter. As usual it had been printed on plain white paper, and the police had already said it could have been printed on any one of two million computer printers in Paris. Pierre leaned over Oscar's shoulder and they silently read the letter together. It read as follows:

Monsieur Oscar Dubois
Editor
Le Figaro

*You asked me in your newspaper why I am doing
these things? I have thought long and hard about this
and I have decided it is time to answer your question.
My name as you already know is Mrs Borgert, and I
was very briefly married to Mr Borgert. We flew to
Paris straight from our wedding and wishing to be
anonymous and left alone, we booked into a fairly
nondescript hotel using a false name. On our second
night we dined at one of Paris's top restaurants, after
which having returned to the hotel my husband
collapsed with severe food poisoning. A doctor was
summoned immediately, but he took forever to appear,
and by the time he did eventually arrive, my poor
husband having been in absolute agony for over one
and a half hours had died. The police were also
summoned straight away and when they eventually
arrived they immediately wrote it off as an 'accidental
death'.*

*To my mind and as far as I am concerned, my
husband's death was not an accident, but the result of
complete and utter negligence by the chef and the
restaurant's management. The same is true of the lack
of medical care - severe negligence and a thoroughly
lackadaisical attitude by the attending doctor and the
medical profession he represents, and a totally
disinterested, couldn't care less attitude by the Paris
police who were not in the least bit interested in
pursuing the people responsible for my wonderful*

husband's death.
Therefore I have taken it upon myself to avenge his death.

This entire incident is typical of the 'better than thou' attitude of France as a country, and in particular of the people of Paris. You do not care about anyone other than yourselves, because you all think you are better than the rest of us, and so yes, I blame the people of Paris.
You asked me why - now you know.

Mrs Borgert

'Wow' said Pierre. 'She really hates us all. Are you going to print it?'

'Of course' replied Oscar 'but I guess I better show it to Claude Dubois and the pair from Interpol first.'

Oscar rang Claude Dubois and Claude then rang us. We all arrived in Oscar's office within fifteen minutes of receiving the summonses. We all read the letter and sat in silence for a moment or two. Sam and I looked at each other and both knew what the other was thinking without saying a word. Do we share what we know? Sam shook her head imperceptively and I gently nodded my agreement. I was pretty sure nobody noticed.

'It's all very interesting' said Hugo 'and I can see why she's so pissed off with everyone, but does it help us find her and stop her?'

'Well' I began 'if they booked into the hotel under a false name, then no doubt the death of her husband was registered under that same false name, and we have no idea what that name is or which hotel they stayed in.'

'Can we talk to all the hotels and ask them if they've had a death from food poisoning in the last few months?' asked Pierre.

'There are over two thousand hotels in Paris' replied Claude 'and if the hotel allowed them both check in under false names without producing any ID, then they are not the sort of establishment that is going to report a death on their premises. No, I'm afraid that's a dead end.'

'Well how about finding the doctor involved?' Oscar asked Claude?'

'If I was the doctor who'd taken so long to arrive that the patient died, I would definitely keep that information to myself. That's going to be another dead end I'm afraid.'

'Do we know which restaurant was involved?' asked Pierre. 'I'm assuming it was 'Cuisine Raffinée' on the Champs-Élysées and Michelle Andre was the chef'.

'Not necessarily' I said. 'If I was Mrs

Borgert I'd definitely not go back to where my husband was poisoned. I'd take my revenge on a totally different restaurant to throw the authorities off the scent. After all, it wasn't the chef she poisoned, but innocent diners.'

'God, this is hard' mused Pierre.

'Welcome to the wonderful world of police work' said Claude.

Louise had been up for about an hour, but was still dressed in her red silk dressing gown covered in gold and silver dragons. It had been a present from Matthias that he'd bought for her in Dubai during their courting days. The dressing gown was now one of her most prized possessions. She thought about the day ahead and whether it was going to be just a reconnaissance day or an action day. That very much depended on what she found when she got to 57 Rue Saint-Jacques. Louise had a shower, did her make-up and then dressed in her favourite outfit, smart denim jeans, a white polo neck top and this time a dark blue zip fronted suede jacket. With a pair of sun glasses on she was sure Dr Gaspard Boucher would not recognize her as the bereft woman crying her eyes out in a three star hotel four months ago. As per usual, now we was dressed as Gemma, she was now thinking as Gemma, and to that end she took a syringe she had previously loaded with strychnine and putting it inside a hard shell spectacles case, she dropped it in her handbag. Before she headed off to Rue Saint-Jacques she had one stop to make, at the sex shop near her secret apartment. She felt sure they would have what she needed.

Gemma arrived in Rue Saint-Jacques and started to walk up the long steady hill. Number 57 was on the right, and a plaque to the side of the door confirmed that this was the surgery for Dr Gaspard Boucher. After a brief pause to catch her breath she pulled on a pair of clear latex gloves, opened the door and walked into the reception. The reception was empty and there was no sign of a receptionist, however, the door to the examination room was open and she could see Dr Boucher sitting at his desk. As soon as he spotted Gemma he got up out of his chair and started walking towards the door, but Gemma got there first, walked into the examination room and closed the door behind her.

'Excuse me Miss, but do you have an appointment?' he asked.

'No doctor, but as I saw the surgery was

empty and there was no receptionist I just walked straight through. I'm sorry if that was wrong.'

Gemma sounded very apologetic and started to turn round.

'Well, you're here now' he said 'and my receptionist has telephoned me to say she is going to be quite late as her child minder is sick, and she now needs to find someone else to look after her daughter before she can come in, so I guess I'll have to manage. Please Miss er?'

'Oh, Miss Carstairs, Emily Carstairs' said Gemma thinking of a name quickly. Mm, no receptionist arriving for quite some time thought Gemma. She decided there and then, today would be an action day.

'Please Miss Carstairs, sit down and how can I help you?'

'Well I have a sharp pain in my left ankle' she said pointing at the offending area 'and I wondered if you would be so kind as to have a look at it for me. It's a really sharp pain and it hurts like hell.'

'Of course' he said standing up. Dr Boucher walked round the desk and bent down in front of Gemma, and slipped her left shoe off. This was exactly what she wanted. She'd already spotted a very large circular glass ashtray on his desk which she reached out for and picked up with her right hand. It was very heavy, and ideal for what she wanted.

'I can't see anything specific' the doctor said looking up into Gemma's face.
He was just in time to see the ashtray speedily approaching his head. He tried to duck out of the way, but he was too slow and the lump of heavy glass crashed into his head knocking him out. Gemma immediately jumped up and rushed over to the door, locking it with the key already in the lock. She then dragged Dr Boucher's unconscious body over to the wall radiator where she used two pairs of the half a dozen hand cuffs she had bought an hour or so earlier at the seedy sex shop. She spread his body out, face up, like a crucifix and handcuffed each wrist to the pipes either side of the radiator. She then took out the syringe and waited for the doctor to regain consciousness. He eventually came round after fifteen minutes, tried to move and then realised he was secured to the radiator.

'What the hell?' he began. 'Who are you and what do you want. Release me straight away, and I won't report this to the police.'

'No, I'm afraid not Dr Boucher. As for my name, well you've probably heard of me. The people of Paris know me as Mrs Borgert, and we have met once before when you attended the death of my husband from food poisoning. You could have saved his life, but you took so long to arrive he died in agony, because you never arrived in time.'

'That could not be helped. I was attending another patient who was seriously injured in a traffic accident. I can't be in two places at once.'

'No, but when you realized you couldn't arrive you should have asked another doctor to attend, but no, you just let my husband die in absolute agony.

Now it is your turn to die in agony.'

Gemma took the syringe out of her glasses case and held it up to show the doctor it was full.

'Do you know what this is?' she asked.

'Obviously not' he replied 'it could be anything.'

'Well as you may well have read, I have so far killed seventeen people using either cyanide or thallium, and their deaths have been quite satisfying, but nowhere near as satisfying as your death will be. I decided those two poisons were too good for you. You let my husband die an agonizing death, and I have decided to treat you to a death in the most agonizing means possible. Strychnine.'

Dr Gaspard Boucher was very familiar with

most poisons and he knew the fate that awaited him if she managed to inject him. He had to stop her, but he could not use his hands or arms. He decided his only option was to try and kick her when she came close, and ideally kick the syringe out of her hand so that it smashed.

'Now tell me Dr Boucher, are you going to accept your fate like a man, or are you going to struggle so that I have to knock you out again?'

'Bitch' he sneered back at her.

'Now, now doctor, that's not a very nice bedside manner is it, calling your patients horrible names. You should be ashamed of yourself. So, what's it going to be, easy or another tap on the head.'

'If you're going to do it, just get on with it' he said through clenched teeth.
Gemma picked up the syringe and walked towards him. Just as she started to bend down to inject him, his right leg swung across viciously towards her trying to kick her in the head. Gemma was half expecting it and rolled away from him so that all he managed to kick was fresh air.

'I gave you the chance to play nicely, but you now leave me no choice.'
Gemma picked up the ashtray and walked

towards him. Dr Boucher struggled and kicked, but Gemma stamped hard down on his leg with her right foot, and as he cried out in pain his concentration momentarily left Gemma and went to his leg. It was all the opportunity she needed. She swung the ashtray at his head again and it smashed into his forehead. He was severely dazed, but just about conscious. Gemma ripped off the left sleeve of Dr Boucher's shirt and then walked over to the desk and picked up the syringe from where she'd left it. She very carefully took off the hypodermics protective cover and dropped it into her handbag, then checking he was still dazed she quickly injected the full contents of the syringe into his arm. Part of her wanted to stop and watch the agony he was about to endure until he died, but common sense prevailed and after ten minutes Gemma collected her belongings and left by a back door leaving Dr Gaspard Boucher to die in total agony, just as her poor Matthias had.

Chapter Nineteen.

Detective Chief Inspector Claude Moreau picked up the phone on his desk, less out of interest and more to stop the incessant ringing. He was not in a good mood.

'Yes' he yelled into the receiver 'What is it?'

He listened and then shouted for Hugo to join him in his office.

'Grab your coat Hugo, it looks like she's struck again.'

'Oh God' he said 'How many this time?'

'Just the one apparently, a doctor with a surgery on Rue Saint-Jacques.'

They both grabbed their jackets and ran down to the car park. En route Claude telephoned me and asked Sam and I to join them at 57 Rue Saint-Jacques. We arrived shortly after the two policeman, and as we showed our Interpol badges to the uniformed policeman on the door, Claude came out and beckoned us into the examination room. Dr Gaspard Boucher lay stretched out on the floor, his thin body contorted into a terrible shape with his back severely arched and a look of complete terror on his face. He still had handcuffs on both wrists still attached to the radiator pipes, and dried blood had obviously run from his forehead down his cheek.

'Any thoughts doctor?' Claude asked Sam.

'Without a thorough examination I can't

be sure' said Sam 'but from the position of his body and the look of horror on his face I'd say he's received a massive dose of strychnine. It's the only poison I know that contorts a body like that.'

'First cyanide, then thallium and now strychnine' mused Claude aloud. 'Where the hell does the bloody woman get this stuff from, you can't exactly buy it over the counter at a high street pharmacy?'

'At a guess I'd say the internet.' I replied. 'I was looking on the net last night and there are numerous companies selling all these poisons, no questions asked. You have to pay really crazy prices of course, but they'll sell you absolutely anything you want. China, Thailand, Afghanistan, Pakistan, Bulgaria, Albania, Rumania. This stuff is available from over twenty different countries, all black market and totally illegal in most central European countries of course, but it's all relatively easy to obtain if you're not too bothered about breaking the law.'

'So why the complete change of direction' asked Hugo 'from the previous random massed poisonings to one very specific and very brutal poisoning?'

'I would think this one was personal' mused Claude.

'If you recall her last letter' said Sam 'in which she described why she was doing all these killings, there was a doctor who she blamed because he took forever to arrive when her husband was poisoned, and if you remember in that letter she said her husband died in absolute agony. Judging by the look on his face and the contortions of his body, this poor man also died in absolute agony. In my humble opinion this was a personal moment of revenge, and this could well be that doctor.'

'That makes a lot of sense' I mused.

'I agree' said Claude. 'But if that is the case and she has now started on the specific individuals, then next on her list must be the chef who she accused of showing complete and utter negligence, and I guess the restaurant's manager who allowed him to do it, according to Mrs Borgert anyway.'

'The trouble is' I said, thinking aloud 'we don't know which restaurant they went to for their meal that evening, and in all probability the restaurant themselves aren't even aware that there was a problem, and a death from food poisoning.'

'Perhaps we could visit all the restaurants in Paris' said Sam 'and warn them to be on the lookout. Actually, thinking about it, do we know how many restaurants there are in Paris?'

'Well it depends on how you define a restaurant' replied Claude. 'According to World Cities Culture Forum, and I only know this because I looked it up yesterday, Paris currently has 44,896 eating establishments, and so no Sam, we can't go and visit each one and warn them. The only person that knows which of the roughly 45,000 is the offending restaurant is Mrs Borgert, and I think she is unlikely to tell us.'

'I have never before been involved in such a frustrating case' said Hugo 'and with so many dead ends. We just can't seem to get ahead of the game, and all we're ever doing is clearing up after the wretched woman.'

'Oh you will get used to it my young friend' lamented Claude. 'When you've been doing this as long as I have you'll find this situation is not all that unusual. We'll get a break eventually, but at the moment I haven't a clue where from. There are no CCTV cameras overlooking the surgery, so we don't know who came through the door, and as far as we can tell nobody else was here at the time.'

'So what do we do now Claude?' asked Sam.

'Well the forensic team have just arrived, so we'll leave them in peace. Believe it or not there are other crimes still going on in Paris and I have to try and deal with them now. I'll give you two a ring and an update as soon as I news on the forensics.'

Sam and I headed back to our hotel, collapsed in a couple of chairs and went over everything we knew so far to see if we'd missed anything.

'Well firstly I guess' started Sam 'there are the things we know from our UK trip that we haven't shared with the French police yet.'

'And don't intend to' I said 'at least, not yet. Like for example we're pretty sure that Mrs Borgert was originally Mrs Gemma Louise Smith and she married a German surgeon named Matthias Borgert.'

'And we know from the vicar's wife' said Sam 'that they flew straight to Paris for their honeymoon, which for me confirms we are right in our suspicions.'

'We know the date of the wedding' said Sam thinking out loud 'so it follows that Matthias Borgert died two days later. Yes?'

'Agreed, but does that necessarily help us? I asked.
Neither of us knew the answer to my question, but as we sat and pondered it, a really silly thought entered my head. I immediately

dismissed it, but the thought just wouldn't go away.

'Sam' I slowly began 'please excuse my thinking on this, and I don't want to upset you, but I can't get the thought out of my head.'

'Go on' she said tentatively, wondering what was coming next.

'If we are in agreement that Mrs Borgert's maiden name before she got married was originally Gemma Louise Smith, then is it just a coincidence that Lady Louise Hamilton Smythe checked into the Four Seasons around the same time the murders began. I don't know, Lady Louise Smythe, Gemma Louise Smith? I just hate coincidences and it doesn't seem possible knowing Louise as we do, but I can't get rid of the thought. What do you think?'

'Good grief Michael' said Sam 'It must be just a coincidence, I can't see or even imagine Louise killing a fly, never mind murdering eighteen people.'

'But she came from England to Paris at the same time as Mrs Borgert did' I argued 'and apart from a slight spelling difference their names are the same. I'm sorry Sam but it really bothers me.'

'OK' Sam allowed, obviously humouring me 'so just suppose for a minute you're correct and Lady Louise is our serial killer, what do you want to do about it?'

'Follow her, see where she goes and what she does, and if possible have a good look round her hotel suite.'

'She'd spot us a mile off and neither of us is a burglar.' said Sam.

'No, but Martin is. We could ring Helena and ask if we could enlist his help.'

'You're really serious about this aren't you?' asked Sam.

'I am' I replied 'and I'm sorry if it feels uncomfortable. I really like Louise, and I certainly don't want her to be our mysterious serial killer, but I think it would be irresponsible of us not to check her out as much as possible.'

'OK, I guess that's fair enough' agreed Sam. 'Why don't you give Helena a call and see if Martin is available?'

The Martin in question was an Interpol officer named Martin Smith. At least, that's the name we all know him by, although he told us a couple of years ago that Smith is not his real name, although Martin is!
We first came across Martin about four years ago when Helena's boss, the current Interpol Commissioner - Kurt Meisner, sent Martin to

help us break into some offices in the middle of the night during a case we were working on in the Bahamas. Martin had for many years been a highly successful burglar in South Africa, but on one particular job about ten years ago, one of the people working with him thought Martin was being over cautious, ignored his strict directions thinking he knew better and in the process set off a silent alarm. Kurt, the Head of Interpol in South Africa at the time caught them all, including Martin, but knowing of Martin's experience and expertise he offered him a choice. Several years in prison or work for Interpol using his extraordinary skills for good, instead of for his own pocket.

Martin took the offer and has now been with Interpol nearly ten years. Sam and I have worked with Martin on several cases and he has become a good friend. Watching Martin in action is like watching a master criminal at work, except of course he now works for us, and I cannot speak highly enough of him.

I telephoned Helena and explained the situation regarding my suspicions about Lady Louise. She said Martin had nothing urgent on his desk at the moment that couldn't wait a week or two, so she would arrange for Martin to catch the KLM evening flight from Amsterdam to Charles de

Gaulle airport in Paris. We offered to meet him, but Martin insisted on us not being seen with him in public, and he would see us in our hotel room the following morning.

Sam and I were staying at the Novotel Tour Eiffel Hotel, a 4 star tourist hotel located on Quai de Grenelle which as its name suggests overlooks the Eiffel Tower. It was very comfortable and we had managed to secure a large double. Helena booked a room in the same hotel for Martin, and at 8.30 am the following morning Martin knocked on our hotel room door. I opened it:

'Good God Michael' he began 'You're still as ugly as ever. How on earth did you manage to hook that beautiful blonde I see across the room?'

'And you don't improve with age, what are you now, mid 70's?'
We both laughed and hugged each other, it was that sort of relationship. Sam came over and joined in the hugs and we all went and sat, Martin and Sam in the two armchairs and I perched on the end of the bed.

'OK guys' began Martin. He always called Sam and I guys, but it was meant affectionately. 'Tell me what you need me to do, but some

background information first please.'
We proceeded to tell Martin about the murders of seven diners using cyanide, then four doctors using thallium, then six police officers using thallium again, and most recently just one doctor using strychnine. We filled him in on the letters Mrs Borgert had been sending to Le Figaro, and we then got to our trip to the UK. I continued:

'Sam and I flew over to the UK to check with the births, deaths and marriages office in Southport to see if there was any record of a fairly recent marriage of a Mr and Mrs Borgert.'

'We knew from her most recent letter' said Sam 'that they'd only been married 48 hours when Mr Borgert died, so it had to be a recent marriage.'

'OK' said Martin. 'I'm with you so far.'

'Much to our delight' I continued 'the department had just received a record from a small church in Worcestershire listing the marriage of a Miss Gemma Louise Smith to a Mr Matthias Borgert. We decided to visit the vicar, a Revd. Arthur P. Featherstone, and just as we were leaving the vicar's wife told us the happy couple had told them they were flying straight to Paris for their honeymoon. The timings fitted exactly.'

'That' said Sam 'more or less confirmed

for us that the very mysterious Mrs Borgert was in all probability Miss Gemma Louise Smith, although we still don't know who she is or where to find her.'

'Hopefully' I said 'that's where you come in'.

'My beloved husband' interrupted Sam 'has a crackpot theory which I find unbelievable, but we are hoping you can throw some light on it and prove him either right or wrong.'

'OK' mused Martin smiling at us both. 'Explain please.'

'Since we have been in Paris, we have met and become very friendly with a certain Lady Louise Hamilton Smythe, who I believe could possibly be Mrs Borgert. We know Mrs Borgert's Christian name and surname were Louise Smith, and the woman we met here is Lady Louise Smythe.'

'A bit of a coincidence Sam' said Martin.

'But you don't know her Martin' argued Sam. 'Lady Louise is really nice, great company to be with and I can't believe she has an evil bone in her body. No, Michael just has to be wrong.'

'Mm' mused Martin 'I can see you really like this Lady Louise Sam, but then again I'm told John George Haigh, the notorious acid bath serial killer was very nice to know and a really generous man to everyone he met. But he killed nine people.'

'So what do we do then?' asked Sam.

'You two do nothing' answered Martin 'Just point her out to me and I'll do the rest. I'll start by following her, and see if she acts suspiciously at all. Then if necessary I'll let myself into her hotel room and have a snoop around.'

'It's not a hotel room' I said 'It's a suite of rooms on the fourth floor of the Four Seasons Hotel King George V'.

'Oh, very posh' mocked Martin. 'Do we know if this Lady Louise is a real lady, or just uses a posh form of address she's not really entitled to?'

'Again, we don't know' I answered 'She doesn't really mention her own background much, although she did say once that her parents have a large house and grounds in Berkshire. She's actually registered at the hotel as Lady Louise Hamilton Smythe.'

'OK' said Martin 'I'll see what I can find out and get back to you.'

Chapter Twenty

Lady Louise was planning the next move. She was pleased with what Gemma had done to Dr Gaspard Boucher, and she now actually thought of Gemma as a different person. Gemma was doing these things in order to revenge her poor dead husband, whereas she, Lady Louise, was just innocently looking on at what Gemma was doing. It was really strange, and she even realised it herself, but she was now able to totally compartmentalize the actions and two sides of the same person. She laughed to herself as she realized what pleasure a psychiatrist would have trying to sort her out. With eighteen deaths now behind her, she now realised for the first time that just two more were needed to complete her task. The chef and the restaurant owner.

Martin was sitting in a very comfortable armchair in the main reception area of the Four Seasons waiting to see if Lady Louise appeared. He had a coffee in front of him and to all intents and purposes, he was busy reading the Daily Telegraph. He had searched the internet the night before, and after an hour or so he had discovered that Lady Louise Hamilton Smythe was the only daughter of Lord Charles Hamilton Smythe and Lady Emily Hamilton Smythe. So at least Louise was a legitimate lady.

The internet also had quite a lot of information on her parents, their background and the family, and thankfully it included several photographs of Lady Louise. Martin had telephoned Michael and told him he didn't need their help in pointing her out after all, and today would be day one of following Lady Louise, assuming of course that she actually went out anywhere.

Now dressed in her 'Gemma' clothes of jeans, smart top and casual jacket, Gemma was deciding on her next move. Fortunately nobody knew which restaurant Gemma and Matthias had eaten at on that fateful evening, and so she could go back there any time without raising suspicion. Gemma needed to know two things, one, if the chef that poisoned Matthias was still the chef, and secondly who actually owned the restaurant? The restaurant in question was actually called 'Seulement le meilleur' which translated as 'Only the best'. Gemma thought about what had sadly happened there and laughed to herself at the inaccuracy of the restaurant's name. She was about to leave when a thought occurred to her. Why go all the way there when she can quite easily find out exactly what she needs to know with a simple telephone call. Gemma picked up her mobile and typed 'Paris restaurant Seulement le meilleur into the search engine. Within two seconds she had the telephone number which she jotted down on the pad sitting on the coffee table in front of her.

Gemma dialled the number and after two rings a man's voice answered the phone.

'Bonjour, Seulement le meilleur. Je suis monsieur Pierre, le Maître d.'

'Ah good morning Monsieur' replied Gemma 'please excuse me but do you by any chance speak English?'

'Of course madam, I also speak Spanish, Italian and German.'

'Well thank you' replied Gemma thinking what a pompous pig she was talking to on the other end of the phone. 'Tell me please monsieur, I came to your excellent restaurant about four months ago and had a superb meal, and I wondered if you still had the same chef?'

'Yes indeed we do madam, we are proud to say Maestro Raphael D'Aurevilly has been our executive chef here at 'Seulement le meilleur' for over six years.'

'Oh excellent' said Gemma 'you won't believe how thrilled I am to hear you say that. Tell me monsieur, who actually owns the restaurant, I would like to present them with a small gift of thanks when I next come for a meal, which will hopefully be this evening if you can squeeze me in?'

'The owner of 'Seulement le meilleur' is Baron Francois Leblanc who bought the restaurant after the death of his wife just over six years ago. Incidentally madam, we prefer not to use the term 'having a meal', instead we encourage our clients to describe dining here as receiving a totally unique gastronomic experience.'

'Oh of course, and how right you are. Tell me monsieur Pierre, can you accommodate four of us this evening, around 8.00 pm?'

'It will be our pleasure madam. What name should I reserve the table in?'

'That will be Lord and Lady Fortescue and our two guests.'

'Excellent my Lady, we shall look forward to seeing you this evening.'

No you won't thought Gemma as she put the phone down. So, now I know the chef's name and the owner. Now all I need to do is find the best opportunity.

Martin was to say the least getting bored, and he was also starting to get strange looks from some of the hotel's reception staff. He'd been sitting in reception for over two hours with no sign of Lady Louise. Martin decided to leave the hotel, and he crossed the road and spent the next couple of hours getting bored in a street café from where he could see the front of the hotel. He dug out his mobile from his jacket pocket and telephoned Sam.

'Hi Sam and good morning to you and Michael. Any chance if you can ring your mate Lady Louise and discreetly try and find out if she is planning on leaving the hotel today? After four hours of watching the front of the hotel I'm to put it mildly bored out of my brain.'
Sam laughed.

'I'll give her a call and see what I can do.'
Sam dialled Louise's mobile.

'Louise Hamilton Smythe' said a cheery voice.

'Hi Louise, it is Sam.'

'Oh, hi Sam and good morning.'

'Look, I just wondered if you had any plans for today, you know, visit an art gallery, have a look round an exhibition, go to a concert, a ballet or an opera, go to see a musical or the theatre, or even have a nice meal somewhere, although I guess that's a bit unsafe these days? As you might have guessed Michael and I are bored.'

'Well I had no plans to go out at all today, but we could meet up for a few drinks if you like. There's a really nice bar with a decent live jazz trio not far from the Four Seasons. I could meet you in reception in say half an hour?'

'Sounds fun, we'll be there.'

Sam hung up and immediately called Martin.

'We're meeting Lady Louise in the hotel's reception in half an hour, and then we're going for a drink in a nearby jazz bar. You can watch us and make sure you recognize Louise, and then after about ten minutes, telephone me and say Michael and I are needed by the police, something to do with the poisonings. We'll rush off and leave you to follow Louise to your heart's content.'

'Sounds perfect Sam. You know you and Michael ought to do this sort of thing for a living!'

'Bye Michael.' said Sam and she hung up.

'Did I just hear you say we are going for a drink with Louise in a jazz bar? Do you really hate me that much?' I asked.

'Oh stop whinging dear' said Sam 'I know you hate jazz, but Louise chose it, and anyway, Martin will ring and call us away after ten minutes. You never know, Louise may do something suspicious, or she may just go back to the Four Seasons.'

We headed over to the Four Seasons and arrived in the reception area just as Louise emerged from a lift. I didn't recognize her at first as she was wearing jeans and a zip up suede jacket, whereas I'd only ever seen her wear very elegant dresses before.

'Hi you two' she began warmly. 'Great idea of yours Sam, I needed to get out of the hotel suite and do something.'

'Actually it was your idea to go for a drink if I remember rightly' Sam replied.

'Oh well, I knew it was one of us' said Louise laughing.

We left the Four Seasons and walked about half a mile to a small bar where you could hear a jazz trio of piano, bass and drums playing inside. Normally I hate jazz, but I have to be honest and admit that they sounded quite good. We went inside and a minute later Martin came in and sat at a different table about twenty feet away. The three of us sat chatting about anything and everything other than the poisonings for about ten minutes when Sam's mobile rang. She answered and spoke to Martin who was on the other end.

'Bonjour Mademoiselle' he began 'This is

Chief Inspector Clouseau of the French Police, and I have to inform you that you are under arrest for looking far too attractive and putting people off of their drinks.'

'Oh, OK Chief Inspector' said Sam trying her hardest not to laugh 'Michael and I will be there as soon as possible.'

Sam cut off the call and glanced over at Martin who was smiling at her. Sam ignored him and said:

'That was Detective Chief Inspector Moreau, he would like us to meet him straight away. Something to do with the poisonings, but he didn't say what.'

'I guess we better head off then' I said. 'I'm sorry Louise, but we have no choice. Stay and finish your drink. The trio are quite good. We'll give you a call later if it's anything interesting.'

'Mm, that would be good' said Louise. 'Catch up later.'

We left the bar and headed back to our own hotel.

Louise now sat in the bar on her own, listening to the gentle music of the jazz trio, slowly sipping her gin and tonic and wondering what to do. Should she go back to the hotel or as she was already out, should she perhaps do a bit of recognisance on 'Seulement le meilleur', the restaurant where her husband's killer still worked. She decided on the latter as she thought a good walk would probably do her good, and she needed to check the back door of the restaurant as well as the front. Martin still sat at his table slowly sipping a shandy, he never drank when he was working, and he continued to discretely watch Louise.

After about ten to fifteen minutes, Louise got up, left a twenty euro note under her glass and walked out of the bar. Martin was out and behind her a minute later. Louise turned right and began heading up the gentle slope of the road they were on, Martin immediately crossed over and followed her from the other side of the road. After half a mile or so, Louise turned right into a very up market residential area of Paris and carried on walking up yet another slight slope. Martin did the same, but still keeping to the opposite side of the road to Louise. After another half a mile or so, a few bars and restaurants started to appear and Louise slowed her pace. Martin did the same. He was about forty yards or so behind her. Louise arrived outside a very smart looking restaurant and taking out her mobile phone she took a couple of photographs of the front of the restaurant. Martin just watched her from a distance, doing nothing that might attract attention. Looking around her, Louise then walked back in the direction she'd come from for about twenty yards, and then turned into a side alley. Martin quickly ran across the road to ensure he didn't lose sight of her. Louise had emerged into a back road that ran parallel with the main road she had left. Martin ducked behind a large green rubbish skip where he could watch her without being seen himself. Louise walked about twenty yards up the road, stopped, looked to her left and then her right, and being pretty sure she was unobserved, she took a photograph of the back of the same restaurant. She walked another ten yards and then took another photograph. Louise then walked back past the restaurant and ten yards later stopped and took another photograph of the back of the restaurant. Martin was well hidden and stayed that way as he watched as Louise head back to the main road and then retrace her steps heading back down the slope. Martin saw where she was going and before following her he quickly took a photograph himself of both the front and the back of the same restaurant and then from about sixty yards away he followed Louise all the way back to the Four Seasons hotel.

Chapter Twenty One

Martin telephoned us to make sure we were at our hotel and then said he would join us in our room in about ten minutes.

'Well I don't know if she's your poisoner or not' began Martin 'but I've just spent the last hour and a half or so following her, and her behaviour I have to say I found quite strange.'

'In what way?' asked Sam

'Well after you two left the bar, she sat staring at her drink for ten minutes, obviously deep in thought and I would guess trying to make a decision about something or other. Then she suddenly gulped down what was left of her drink, got up and left the bar. I followed her from the opposite side of the road. She walked about a mile eventually arriving in an upmarket area of very smart houses, restaurants and bars. She seemed to know exactly where she was going as she didn't hesitate at all or look up any directions. She eventually arrived at a restaurant called'

Martin looked down at his phone to get the name

'Seulement le meilleur' he said 'and then she took a few moments, looked around and then when she was sure nobody was looking she photographed the restaurant on her mobile phone. Now, the most interesting bit came next.'

'Go on' said Sam intrigued.

'She then walked back about twenty yards or so and walked down an alley and out into a back road behind the restaurant. I hid behind a large rubbish bin and she never spotted me, but again having looked round to ensure she wasn't being watched, she took three photos of the rear entrance from three different angles.'

'It sounds to me' I said 'like our dear friend Lady Louise was staking out the venue of her next poisoning.'

'She could just have been seeing what the restaurant was like before making a booking' suggested Sam 'including that the hygiene standards behind the front façade were up to standard.'

'Oh come on Sam' I said 'You don't believe that any more than I do, and in your heart you know darn well that's not what she was doing.'

'Sorry Sam' said Martin. 'I know you really like her, but I'm afraid I'm with Michael on this one. She was acting very suspiciously and from everything you've told me I would say it's an eighty to ninety percent chance that she's the poisoner. You two know the set up here better than I do, so what next? Do we tell the local police chief and have her arrested?'

'No point' I replied 'There is absolutely zero evidence against her. When the diners at the first restaurant were killed Sam and myself were both there, and Louise we know definitely wasn't. Likewise at the hospital and the police headquarters, nobody saw her and at the time of the deaths she was at the ballet or at a concert etc. There are no fingerprints to check on anything and there is not a scrap of evidence been left behind anywhere. In other words there is zero evidence against her. If she is our poisoner then we need to find some evidence from somewhere, and I hate to say it, but I think we need to catch her in the act.'

'So, do we watch her twenty four seven?' asked Sam.

'I think we have to' answered Martin 'but I can't do that on my own, and no offence but you two can't help as she knows you both. I'll give Helena a ring and see if we can borrow a couple of extra bodies.'

Martin telephoned Helena, and having listened to everything going on here in Paris she decided the Paris poisonings should now take priority, and to that end she said she would fly down to Paris with George, Colin and Jo in the Interpol Gulfstream later today.

'I'll continue to watch her as best I can in the meantime' said Martin 'but I just hope she does nothing straight away.'

Gemma sat in one of the many comfortable armchairs in her suite trying to decide what to do next. 'Maestro Raphael D'Aurevilly' the executive chef at 'Seulement le meilleur' would be easy enough to find every night at the restaurant, but Gemma was not stupid, and she realised restaurants were an obvious targets for the poisoner, and so there was a good chance they were being watched by undercover police. For all she knew every restaurant in Paris was being watched. The killings were still the main story on every front page, and the government may have even called in the army dressed in plain clothes to keep an eye on Paris's restaurants. Gemma sat and thought about what to do next for over an hour, after which she drafted a plan. She then went over it, adapted it, changed bits here and there, and when she was satisfied she then spent the next hour trying to find flaws in it. Hard as she tried she couldn't.

Gemma liked the plan, it should work, and by far and most importantly of all, she should get away with it.

The next task she decided was to write to Le Figaro again and ensure the people of Paris knew she was still around. The death of Dr Gaspard Boucher had not been reported in any of the papers, and she guessed the police were waiting for Mrs Borgert to confess to yet another killing. Gemma decided the time was right, and after thirty minutes at her computer she was happy with the letter. It read:

Monsieur Oscar Dubois
Editor
Le Figaro

To the people of Paris

In my previous letter to this newspaper, I told you how a doctor had been summoned to our hotel immediately my poor husband became ill, but as I previously stated the wretched doctor took forever to appear, and by the time he did eventually arrive, my poor husband having been in absolute agony for over one and a half hours had died. That doctor was Dr Gaspard Boucher, and I use the term 'was' deliberately as Dr Gaspard Boucher is no more. I visited him at his surgery earlier this week, and when he was not expecting it I knocked him unconscious. I then handcuffed him 'crucifix' style to the radiator pipes in his office and injected him with a lethal dose of strychnine. On this occasion I chose to use strychnine as it is by far the most painful of all the poisons, and it is only right that those responsible for the agony my beloved husband went through should be feeling the same level of agony that they had inflicted upon him. I have not yet finished my revenge, so as I have said to the people of Paris before: Be aware, be very aware.

Mrs Borgert

As it happened, Gemma had more or less decided there would be no more random mass killings, just individual targets, but she was enjoying the fear she had put into the minds of millions of Parisians. The next problem was how to get the letter to the editor of Le Figaro. She thought about it for a while and decided she would simply post it. After all, there was no rush. With the stamped envelope safely tucked away in her handbag, Gemma put on a jacket and a pair of leather gloves and went for a leisurely walk. Twenty minutes later she arrived at her intended destination, the Peninsular Hotel on Avenue Kléber. No doubt the letter would be traced back to its source if possible, and that shouldn't be the Four Seasons. Once she'd arrived at the Peninsular she sat in the reception lounge reading a magazine and drinking a couple of coffees for forty or so minutes and then as she was leaving Gemma very discretely dropped the envelope into the hotels mailbox, shielding her action from everyone as much as possible with her body, just in case. Having posted her letter, she took a leisurely walk back to her own hotel.

Unbeknown to Gemma, Martin had been watching her from the moment she got out of the lift and walked into the Four Seasons reception area. As he'd done before he followed her walk from the opposite side of the road, and Martin also sat and drank a couple of coffees on the opposite side of the lounge of the Peninsula when they arrived there. Unfortunately, Martin did not notice Gemma drop the envelope into the Peninsula's mail box. It wasn't that he wasn't watching her, he was, but it was simply the case that Gemma hid her movements extremely well from everyone with her body, just in case.

The following day, Le Figaro's front page headline read:

'L'EMPOISONNIER DE PARIS GRÈVE ENCORE'

which translated into English read:

'THE PARIS POISONER STRIKES AGAIN'

Gemma read it with satisfaction. She was still front page news, and very slowly and bit by bit she felt Matthias was being avenged. The most satisfying by far had been the death of the awful Doctor Gaspard Boucher, which after she had injected the strychnine, she had hung around fascinated to watch the agony start for about ten minutes before leaving. She had heard him cry out in agony, and in order to shut him up she had gagged him with his own shirt sleeve which she'd ripped of his left arm. Having seen how effective it was Gemma had also decided that her next victim, 'Maestro Raphael D'Aurevilly' the executive chef at 'Seulement le meilleur' would also die by strychnine poisoning. She had a quiet afternoon in her suite and after her evening meal, delivered by room service, she took out the plan which she had typed up and kept with her diary in the hotel wall safe located inside her wardrobe, and she took out both. The diary was kept up to date on a daily basis as

Gemma entered all the day's thoughts, plans and events when she got into bed every night. She entered all today's activities and her thoughts into the diary, then Gemma read through the plan for Raphael D'Aurevilly once more, smiled to herself, put out the bedside lamp and went to sleep.

Chapter Twenty Two

Sam and I were sitting waiting with a couple of coffees in the private VIP section of Charles de Gaulle international airport where Interpol's Gulfstream 650 had just landed and taxied to a halt. We showed our Interpol badges to the security staff at the exit, walked over to the jet, and the second the stairs were lowered we climbed aboard the aircraft we'd grown to know so well during our adventures breaking the Cairo Conspiracy. Helena and Sam threw their arms around each other as usual and I received bear hugs from both George and Colin, the two Interpol pilots. Jo, the resident stewardess was looking as gorgeous as ever and the six of us sat down in the aircrafts extremely comfortable lounge area while Sam and I brought everyone up to date. Helena, despite only being in her thirties was Interpol's European Head of

Operations, George and Colin, as well as being top pilots were both very senior Interpol Inspectors and undercover officers, and Jo was also, despite her cat walk model appearance, a very experienced undercover operative holding the rank of Sergeant.

'So what exactly do you need from us?' asked Helena.

'I firmly believe we now know exactly who Mrs Borgert, ie 'The Paris Poisoner' as 'Le Figaro' has nicknamed her, is in fact Lady Louise Hamilton Smythe. Sam disagrees with me, although I think she knows in her heart of hearts it's true but she doesn't want to admit it she really likes Louise.'

'Yeah, I guess that's fair enough' said Sam.

'The main problem is that there is zero evidence against her, or anyone else for that matter. There are no fingerprints, Louise was always in company with lots of witnesses at the time of the killings and as you all know without evidence we can do nothing. Martin followed her all day yesterday, and he believes she was acting suspiciously, although he doesn't know why. So to sum up, we need Louise Hamilton Smythe under twenty four hour surveillance, without her knowing she's being watched.'

'Is this Louise woman good looking?' asked Colin.

'Yes, very. Why?' asked Sam.

'Oh' he answered 'I only try to watch or work with extremely good looking women, that's why I've got this job with all you lovely ladies.'

'Are you after a promotion again?' laughed Helena 'because with sexist comments like that you're more likely to be demoted than promoted. You know how terribly sensitive poor Jo is, as are Sam and myself.'

'Yes' said Jo 'and I still have a very good right hook my Irish friend.'

'Oh begorrah and begosh' said Colin putting on his broad Irish accent 'if I offended your delicate feelings ladies then this Irish idiot doth truly agolopise.'

'Deliberately mispronouncing words isn't helping your cause Colin' suggested George smiling. 'Can I suggest you indulge in a prolonged period of reflective silence?'

'Where is Martin now?' asked Helena getting back to the serious business.

'He was sitting in the lounge facing reception at the Four Seasons, Louise's hotel waiting to see if she emerged again, but he rang just before you got here to say there's no sign of

Louise, so he's assuming she's turned in for the night, and as he's knackered Martin is also going to bed.'

'OK, fine. I've booked the four of us into the same hotel as you, Sam and Martin' said Helena 'so can I suggest we head over there straight away, draw up a rota and make it a bit easier on Martin tomorrow? Do you by any chance have a photograph of this Lady Louise?'

'Several on my laptop that Martin took during the last twenty four hours' I answered. 'I'll print off copies for everyone.

'Excellent. Now, the last thing. Nobody, including the Paris police must know we are here. It would simply draw attention to Interpol and that's the last thing we need when we're trying to watch someone without them knowing. We are simply four tourists on holiday. So, can I suggest we unload our luggage, grab a couple of taxis and head for the hotel?'

After breakfast the following morning Helena handed out a surveillance rota for the team. She'd deliberately left Sam and I off the rota as Louise would recognize us both a mile away, and Helena also suggested we should get as close to Louise as we possibly could. Knowing we were Interpol officers as she did, she would hopefully be less wary if she thought we suspected nothing. The rota was broken down into four hour shifts, with people operating in pairs. George and Jo were the first pair on duty, and their job was simply to watch and follow Louise until they were relieved by Colin and Martin. Helena was keeping out of sight as much as possible as we'd told her that Detective Chief Inspector Claude Moreau had looked up Helena on the Paris police computer system when he first approached Interpol, and consequently he knew what she looked like.

Lady Louise appeared in the hotel lobby just after 10.30 am. She walked straight out of the door and turned left, heading up the hill. George crossed the road and followed her movements from about twenty yards back, whereas Jo stayed on the same side of the road, but kept about forty yards back. Louise was in no hurry, and stopped to look in a couple of windows as she passed various shops. Eventually she turned left off the main road and headed into a less salubrious part of Paris, but George and Jo kept pace with her. Louise, about thirty yards ahead of George turned another corner, but by the time George arrived there was no sign of her. Jo joined him a few seconds later. They were standing in an open courtyard with three streets heading off in different directions, and several apartment block doors opening into the courtyard.

'So what do we do now?' asked Jo.

'What can we do? George replied. 'You stay here Jo in case she emerges from one of these buildings, and I'll run down each of these streets and see if there's any sign of her.'
George was back fifteen minutes later.

'Anything?' asked Jo.

'Nothing' answered George 'no sign of her. What about you?'

'Likewise, I've only seen two people, an elderly lady came out of that apartment block and went down that street, and an old man came out of the block at the end and went down the street you've just come from.'

'Oh, yes, I passed him on the way back. We're wasting our time here. We just have to go back and admit we've lost her. God knows where she went, but there's no sign of her anywhere. Come on Jo, let's go and face the music.'

Three days earlier, Gemma had gone shopping in an open air junk market. There were several held every week all over Paris where people could sell items they no longer wanted. Gemma had made several purchases, and she took them all straight to the rented apartment she'd used a couple of times previously. Once inside she packed everything into the smart black suitcase she had just purchased, and then carrying the case she headed off towards another apartment she had rented in a different part of Paris. Here she dumped everything in the room she had rented for a month, and again, no questions were asked. They never were in this part of Paris.

Today, as she walked away from the Four Seasons Gemma had an eerie feeling that she was being followed by someone. It wasn't that she'd actually seen anyone, but it was like a sixth sense. She headed towards the new apartment she'd rented just three days earlier, and as soon as she reached the square and turned the corner she ran as quickly as possible through the open front door and up the stairs to the first floor room. She let herself in and then sat on the bed for a minute catching her breath. She wasn't sure if she was being followed or not, but she'd run just be on the safe side. Gemma quickly got changed out of her own clothes, smart black trousers, cream blouse and a blue suede jacket, and she dressed in the clothes she had bought in the market. She'd also bought an old navy blue duffle bag in the market and Gemma transferred the contents of her handbag into the duffle bag. She quickly checked her appearance in the mirror on the front of the wardrobe, opened the door, stepped out, and locking it behind her she slowly walked down the stairs and out into the square. There was a woman hanging about in the square now and she looked totally out of place. She was very smartly dressed and seemed quite agitated. Gemma ignored her and slightly stooping she walked up one of the side streets. She passed a man she didn't recognize in his early forties she estimated coming the other way, and looking back over her shoulder a minute later she saw he'd stopped in the square and was now chatting with the woman. Gemma just smiled to herself and kept walking.

Gemma walked for another twenty minutes and eventually arrived at the address she had obtained three days earlier. Nobody paid her much attention as she looked nothing like the attractive woman who had entered the apartment half an hour earlier. Not only had she changed into all the clothes she had purchased at the second hand market, she had also put on three accessories she had bought the same day at a theatrical costumiers. Those three accessories were a medium length man's wig of grey hair, a grey 'stick on' false moustache, and a pair of light blue tinted gold rimmed spectacles. With the accessories and the selection of men's clothes she had bought and was now wearing, it was no wonder people looking out for an attractive woman wouldn't give an elderly man in a scruffy old coat a second look. When she'd got to the apartment Gemma had stripped off everything apart from her own panties. She flattened her ample bosom with two wide bandages wrapped around her and then held in place with safety pins. She then put on a pair of brown trousers, the old red and grey checked shirt, a brown waistcoat, a pair of black shoes and the dark grey overcoat. Nothing in the ensemble matched, but that was good, it wasn't supposed to. Gemma then tucked her own hair up and forced it all inside the hair net she had bought with the wig. Next she put on the grey wig, and then using spirit gum she glued the matching coloured moustache in place across her top lip. Gemma rubbed some dust and grime into her hands and face, put on the spectacles, and then finished the look with a grubby old workman's cap. With the duffle bag over her shoulder, to all intents and purposes the stooped figure leaving the apartment block was an eighty year old man who everybody just ignored as they'd rushed by.

On the way to her intended destination, Gemma made a short diversion via an art gallery and surprised the clerk on duty by buying a ticket for that afternoon's exhibition. The clerk watched the old man enter, shook his head in wonder and went back to reading his novel. Deep into his book he failed to notice Gemma as she ducked down, crept past his little box office and was back outside less than a minute after arriving. Gemma pocketed the ticket and would visit the exhibition later. The most important thing had been to get the ticket which was happily time and date stamped. Ten minutes later and having now arrived at the private address she had obtained simply by following Raphael D'Aurevilly home after the restaurant closed one evening, she put on a pair of transparent latex gloves, and then walked around to the back of his house. Gemma could hear a vacuum cleaner humming away inside the house and it stopped when she knocked on the back door. A few seconds later a young maid opened it.

'Ah, bonjour mademoiselle' Gemma

spluttered out trying hard to sound gruff and manly. 'Do you speak English by any chance' she asked?

'Yes I do sir, how may I help you?'

'Is Mister Raphael D'Aurevilly at home please' she asked 'I have a private matter to discuss with him?'

The maid simply nodded and disappeared back inside the house, leaving the back door slightly ajar. Gemma quickly entered the house through it and then leant against the wall pretending to be a little faint. As the vacuum cleaner started up again from a room down the hall, Raphael D'Aurevilly appeared from a side door which from the little Gemma could see appeared to be his study. He closed the door behind him as he approached the old man leaning against the wall in front of him.

'Good morning sir, how may I help you?' he said looking concerned.

'Please excuse me' said Gemma in a gruff voice 'I am feeling a little faint. May I sit down please' and as she spoke Gemma pointed at a chair in the hall.

'Of course' replied the chef courteously, and he walked over and picked up the chair. While his back was turned, Gemma reached inside the duffle bag and quickly pulled out a black rubber police style truncheon with a metal core running through it that she had obtained during her visit to the sex shop two weeks earlier. She was still trying to work out in her head why a sex shop would sell such things, but hey ho! Everyone has their vices. She held the cosh behind her back as Raphael brought the chair over and put it next to her. As the chef bent down slightly to position the chair Gemma quickly raised her arm and equally quickly brought it down again, hitting him as hard as she could on the head. He immediately fell to the floor unconscious. The maid had heard nothing because of the sound of the vacuum cleaner loudly humming away in the other room, and Gemma used the opportunity to drag Raphael D'Aurevilly into his own study. Once inside she locked the door, dragged the heavy torso of the man as best she could over to the wall and quickly handcuffed him, arms outstretched to the radiator pipes just as she had done previously with Dr Gaspard Boucher. Gemma wasted no time on waiting for him to come round, and instead reached into the duffle bag again, drawing out a white plastic food container which held a syringe full of strychnine which she had earlier wrapped in several layers of foam rubber and kitchen roll to ensure it didn't break if it rolled around inside the bag. She didn't want to hang around this time as there was someone else in the house, so she immediately pushed the full contents of the syringe into the arm of the unconscious chef, straight through the sleeve of his shirt. She picked up his own handkerchief which was laying on his desk next to a large pale green blotting pad and stuffed it into his mouth. Gemma then unlocked the study door, and hearing the vacuum was still humming away in another room and checking nobody was about, she went out into the hall taking the study key with her. Gemma turned and locked the door of the study behind her, pocketed the key and then quietly let herself out of the back door. Twenty minutes later she was back at the apartment having dropped the chef's study key down a drain en route. Fifteen minutes later after washing and dressing back into her own smart clothes, she left the apartment and quickly walked back to the art gallery, and then after a quick ten minute visit she headed back to the Four Seasons.

Chapter Twenty Three

'I'm so sorry Helena' pleaded George 'but

I don't know what else we could have done. I'm sure she never saw us following her, and I guess she's just very cautious or we were extremely unlucky.'

'Don't worry about it George' answered his boss 'these things happen.'

'What it does prove however is that she was up to no good' said Jo.

'Sorry to argue Jo' I said 'but it proves nothing other than when she turned the corner she disappeared somewhere. She could have gone straight into an already open apartment of a sick friend and closed the door behind her, which was why you never saw her when you arrived in the square.'

'Mm, I see what you mean' said Jo.

'I take your point Michael' said George 'but I don't believe it for a second.'

'Oh I don't believe it either' I said smiling 'but I'm just pointing out the fact that she disappeared from view proves nothing.'

'Colin is still watching out for her in the reception of the Four Seasons' said Helena 'and he'll let us know the minute she returns.'

'You have to hand it to her' said Martin. 'If she is the Paris Poisoner, and I personally think she is, she's been bloody brilliant so far. No witnesses, no finger prints, no clues, no mistakes and so far eighteen dead bodies with probably more to follow. I know this sounds a bit weird and I apologise for saying this out loud, but I kind of admire her.'

'Oh I agree' replied Helena. 'I too appreciate, and to a certain extent admire anyone who excels at their chosen profession. I just don't happen to like Lady Louise Hamilton Smythes current chosen profession.'

'Is everyone saying they are sure Louise is the Paris Poisoner?' asked Sam.

'Yes, I'm afraid so' replied Helena.

'In that case I'm all for catching her and seeing she gets what's coming to her' said Sam. 'She well and truly took me in and she has made a right fool of me. I hate being duped like this, so let's make sure we bring her down.'

'Nice to have you on our side at last' I said smiling.

'Oh I've always been on the same side as everybody else' said Sam 'I guess I was just reluctant to admit it.'

We carried on chatting for another twenty minutes, and then Helena's phone rang.

'Hi boss,' said Colin on the other end of the phone 'she's back at the hotel and has gone straight up to her suite.'

'Thanks Colin' replied Helena. 'Stay put

and I'll have someone come and relieve you in ten minutes.'

Helena cut the phone call and then turned to me, 'Michael, can you and Sam go and call on Louise and see what she claims to have been up to this afternoon, but don't push it, we don't want her to think you're on to her.'

'Will do' I replied, and we left straightaway heading for the Four Seasons.

Gemma was really pleased with her achievements today. She had got her revenge on the chef that had poisoned and killed her dear Matthias, although she was really disappointed that she couldn't stop and watch him die in agony, but her own safety had to take priority. She had lost the couple following her, if that's what they were doing, but she still wasn't sure about that one way or the other, but to be on the safe side she had set up a suitable alibi if it was ever needed. Two days earlier she had made her way to the Piedmont Gallery, a small to medium sized private gallery selling modern works by French artists along with a large selection of sculptures and busts. It was on her way to the Piedmont that she had found the apartment she had taken. The one she'd previously used was fine when she needed to visit Le Figaro's offices in disguise, it was just a three minute walk away, but she'd needed to find somewhere a lot closer to her two intended victims from 'Seulement le meilleur'. Gemma had been walking towards the restaurant when she'd suddenly found herself in an open square with several side streets leading off of it, but far more importantly, there were several open doors of apartment blocks. Gemma had taken a few minutes to pick the one she thought would probably be best for her needs and then she had knocked on the door of the concierge for that particular block. Yes, he did have an apartment she could rent on the first floor, but he'd need two weeks rent paid in advance. Gemma had given him four weeks rent in cash and taken over the apartment immediately getting the key from the concierge. She had then continued her journey to the Piedmont where she'd had a really good look around. She had seen exactly what she wanted, but deliberately did nothing about it leaving without talking to anyone.

Today, on her way back to her hotel after killing Raphael D'Aurevilly and getting changed at the apartment into her own clothes, Gemma had walked back and called in at the Piedmont again. She'd checked on her first visit two days earlier, and as far as she could tell there were no CCTV cameras anywhere. She knocked on the door of the proprietor and explained to him that she'd been in the gallery for over an hour, and after much searching she had eventually found the ideal gift for her father's upcoming birthday. A large white alabaster bust of Sir Winston Churchill on a white marble plinth. Her father had always admired Mr Churchill she told the galleries owner. They agreed a fee and Gemma paid with a credit card in the name of Lady Louise Hamilton Smythe. She obtained a dated receipt and having given the owner her father's name and address in Buckinghamshire and having arranged shipping, she left and quickly headed for the hotel.

The telephone in Gemma's hotel suite rang and she picked it up straight away.

'Lady Louise speaking' she said.

'Oh hi Louise' said Sam 'we weren't sure if you were in or not and we wondered if you fancied a coffee and a cake somewhere?'

'Sounds great' answered Louise. 'How about coming to my hotel suite, I'd love to see you and Michael and have a catch up, but I've been out for what feels like hours and I'm happy to have now stopped, but please join me if you can.'

'Sounds great' replied Sam. 'See you in about fifteen minutes.'
We arrived at the suite of Lady Louise Hamilton Smythe and she opened the door to us herself and gave Sam a kiss on the cheek and beamed at me.

'Excuse my language you two' she began 'but I'm bloody knackered. I seem to have been on my feet all day.'

'What have you been up to then?' I asked.

'Well it's my father's birthday next week, and I had no idea what to get him other than he has recently started collecting a few paintings and one or two bits of sculpture. So I've spent most of the day looking round a few galleries to see if I could find something suitable. I was on my way to see a couple of private galleries the other side of Paris when I turned a corner and came across an elderly lady who had literally collapsed in front of me onto the street just outside her front door. I picked her up and took her inside, made her a hot drink and then once I was sure she was OK I left her, but it was quite worrying for a while.'

'Good grief' I commented 'poor lady. It was a good job you turned up when you did. Where exactly was this?' I asked.

'Oh I've no idea' replied Louise. 'Some apartment block in a square on the way to the gallery, but I've no idea what it was called.'

'So did you get your father something for his birthday?' asked Sam.

'I did in the end' replied Louise. I went to the 'Le Mans Galleria' first and spent about half an hour walking round it, but they had nothing that my father would like, so I left there and went on to the Piedmont Gallery. I must have walked round it for at least an hour, and in the end I found exactly what I wanted, a lovely white alabaster bust of Winston Churchill. My father has always been a fan. Here, look, I took a couple of pictures on my mobile.'

Louise pressed a couple of buttons on her mobile and showed us two pictures, one of the bust and a selfie with Louise and the gallery's owner standing either side of the bust on its plinth.

'To be honest it was a lot more than I wanted to pay' she said, and handed a receipt to Sam with the gallery's name and address on it and confirmation that she'd paid €2,750 euros for the bust, the plinth and shipping to the UK. The receipt was also date stamped with today's date, and clipped to it was her entry ticket, duly time stamped one and a half hours earlier.

As alibi's go, it was a pretty dammed good one.

Lady Louise had written and dated confirmation of where she'd been, what time she'd arrived, a photograph proving it and lastly a witness who would no doubt vouch for her. I hated saying it, but I had to admit, she was bloody good at this.

'Mind you' continued Louise smiling 'I don't begrudge it really, my father is a wonderful man, but I just wish I'd found Mr Churchill when I'd first arrived instead of wandering round for over an hour, then my poor feet wouldn't ache so much.'
We left Louis's hotel suite half an hour later having drunk two pots of tea between us and having eaten numerous freshly baked English style scones with strawberry jam and clotted cream.

'God knows where she's really been' I said 'but I'm afraid her alibi is pretty unbreakable.'
We were back in our own hotel and all gathered in our bedroom. I told everyone else what Louise had told us and was just about to ask what we did next when my mobile rang.
'Michael Turner' I answered.
'Ah, Michael, it is Detective Chief Inspector Claude Moreau. I'm afraid our killer has struck again. A maid has just reported the

death of a Raphael D'Aurevilly. He was the head chef at one of Paris's top restaurants, and from what is being reported to me it looks like another strychnine poisoning. Can you and Samantha please join us as soon as possible?'

He gave us the address and then hung up. I told the rest of our team what he'd said and then asked Helena what she wanted us to do, and should we tell the French police anything about Lady Louise at this stage.

Helena thought about it and then said

'No, well at least, nothing much. You two should go to the address you've just been given and you should tell Claude Moreau something that may help him without interfering with our own enquiries. So far Interpol has been no little or no help whatsoever to the French police, and I think we need to give them something before they stop cooperating with us. I suggest you tell Claude that Interpol has just discovered Mrs Borgert is in fact Mrs Gemma Borgert, and that the husband's name was Matthias, a German surgeon. Tell them no more than that, but hopefully it should be enough to ensure they keep us informed of everything going on.'

Sam and I left straight away and ten minutes later a taxi dropped us outside the home of Raphael D'Aurevilly. We showed out Interpol badges to the gendarme on the front door and went inside. Claude and Hugo were in the study with the body. Like Dr Boucher, the victim was handcuffed to the radiator pipes and his body was incredibly contorted with his back severely arched. A clean white handkerchief had been dropped over his face.

'You don't want to look at his face' said Claude 'It will give you nightmares.'

'One bit of good news from our end' I said. 'I've just heard from Interpol headquarters and having done a lot of investigation into births deaths and marriages they are now one hundred percent certain that Mrs Borgert is Mrs Gemma Borgert, and she was married to a Matthias Borgert, a German surgeon. We know no more than that at this stage, but at least we have a couple of names to work with.'

'Thank you Michael' said Claude. 'That's great news. I must admit I was beginning to wonder if Interpol were ever going to contribute anything to this case, but as it now turns out that is a lot more information than we have managed to dig up ourselves so far.'

'Well I'm not sure how much it will help' I said 'but at least it's a start. As for this poor bugger, looking at the position of the body I don't suppose there's much doubt that it is strychnine poisoning again?' I asked Sam.

'No' she confirmed. 'Definitely the same poison, and definitely the same killer.'

'You say he was a chef?' I asked Claude 'So should I assume he was the chef that poisoned Mrs Borgert's husband, although I suppose we can now refer to him as Matthias Borgert.'

'Yes' said Claude 'a good point.'

'I don't know much knowing their Christian names is going to help' said Hugo 'but it certainly feels better being able to put full names to them. Do we know what nationality Gemma Borgert is?'

'I assume with a name like Gemma she is English?' said Claude inquisitively.

'Yes, that's right, she is, but at this stage I don't have any more information than that. HQ will let me know as soon as they find out anything more, and I'll then pass it straight on to you.'

'Thank you Michael, much appreciated.'

'I suppose we should now expect another letter to Le Figaro?' said Sam.

'Yes' agreed Claude 'but the last one was posted at the Peninsula and I presume the next one will be posted from another hotel, and we can't watch every post box in Paris.'

'Besides' said Hugo 'we may know her name now, but we still don't know what the hell she looks like. Any chance of a passport photo?'

'I don't think so' I replied thinking on my feet as I didn't want to give anything else away. 'From what I gather from HQ she used a false maiden name when they got married and nobody at the church bothered to check it. That's sadly a dead end I'm afraid.'

I wanted to close off that line of enquiry before the French police started digging into UK records. The last thing we needed was them interfering and screwing with our suspicions about Lady Louise. No, it was more than suspicions, we knew it was her, all we had to do now was prove it.

Chapter Twenty Four

Gemma sat at the desk in her hotel suite staring at her laptop. She felt it was time to write to La Figaro again but she wasn't sure how to start the letter or exactly how much information to put in it. In her mind there was just one last killing to complete, that of the restaurant owner Baron Francois Leblanc, and hopefully once he was dead she could let Matthias rest in peace and return to her life in Buckinghamshire.

She wrote several drafts, and then discarded them all as possibly giving away too much information. She eventually settled on the following:

Monsieur Oscar Dubois
Editor
Le Figaro

To the people of Paris

In my previous letter to this newspaper, I told you all about how I made Dr Gaspard Boucher suffer the same agonizing fate that he had previously inflicted on my poor husband with his complete negligence of the Hippocratic Oath. As you are fully aware from my previous communications with you all, that agony was directly caused by the blatant carelessness and obvious negligence of a so called master chef who poisoned my poor husband.

Today I visited that so called executive chef Monsieur Raphael D'Aurevilly at his home, and exactly as I did with Dr Gaspard Boucher, I knocked him unconscious, handcuffed him 'crucifix' style to the radiator pipes in his private study and injected him with a lethal dose of strychnine. As much as I would have liked to, unfortunately I could not stay and watch him suffer and die in the painful agony he deserved as his maid was also in the house at the time.

I hope to be able to report back to you all soon on the excruciating death of my next victim.

Mrs Borgert

It was not her best letter she appreciated, but it did the job. The next problem was how to get it to Oscar Dubois at 'Le Figaro'. The obvious thing to do was to post it again, but obviously using a different hotel's mailbox. But ideally she wanted to see Oscar Dubois' face when he read it, but then she realized that would just be taking too big a chance. So, another visit to another hotel it had to be. This time Gemma selected the Hotel Le Royal Monceau Raffles at 37 Avenue Hoche. It was close to the Arc de Triomphe and she would quite enjoy the walk in the fresh air. As she set off with the letter in her handbag she stopped and looked in several shop windows trying to see if she could spot either the man or the woman she thought was possibly following her yesterday. Helena had also thought of that, so Colin and Martin were now on duty. All three of them eventually ended up drinking coffee in the lounge of the Royal Monceau Raffles, and as she was about to leave Louise made a quick visit to the Ladies toilets. Once inside she saw a maid was just about to leave the toilets, and she asked her if she would be so kind as to drop a letter into the mailbox for her. She offered her twenty euros for doing so and the maid happily obliged pocketing the cash. Louise also left the toilets thirty seconds later, and was just in time to see her letter go into the hotel's mailbox. Satisfied her objective of posting the letter unseen had been achieved, she paid for her coffees, strolled out of the hotel and took a leisurely walk back to her own hotel. After a very pleasant evening meal in her suite, she watched a 'romcom' film on the TV and went to bed.

'Nothing' said Martin reporting back to Helena 'at least nothing we could see. She disappeared into the Ladies loo for five minutes, but then when she came out she just paid her bill and strolled back to her own hotel. You have to hand it to her, she's bloody cool.'

'What about the hotel's mailbox' asked Helena?

'She never went anywhere near it' answered Colin. 'We saw several people drop letters or postcards in it, but as I say, Louise didn't go anywhere near it.'

'But surely she didn't walk all that way for a cup of coffee she could have just as easily have had at her own hotel?' asked Helena thinking aloud.

'Perhaps she just wanted some fresh air' suggested Martin 'went for a stroll, got as far as the Arc de Triomphe and decided she needed a coffee and so went to the nearest decent hotel.'

'Mm, come on Martin' mused Helena. 'Do you believe that?'

'No' he laughed 'of course not, not for a second, but that's what I'd say if I was her and like it or lump it, nobody can prove otherwise. Somehow she must have got someone else to post the letter for her, but I don't know how.'

'She's good isn't she?' said Colin.

'Too bloody good' said Martin through gritted teeth. 'But if we just keep following her she's bound to trip up at some point.'

'Now here's an idea' said Helena. 'Tomorrow morning, why don't we all head down to that square where she lost you, knock on every door and see if anybody recognizes her. We've got several different photographs of Louise, and someone must have seen her. Let's meet in the lounge at 9.00 am sharp and then we'll all head to the square. We'll get the bitch yet.

The following morning, 'Le Figaro' printed Gemma's latest letter on their front page. As usual Detective Inspector Hugo Duchand collected the letter and the envelope from Oscar Dubois and took them straight to forensics. All they could report back later was that as usual it was the same common paper and envelope you could buy anywhere, there were no fingerprints apart from Oscar's, and that it had been posted in the mailbox of the Hotel Le Royal Monceau Raffles at 37 Avenue Hoche.

Claude telephoned me and told me about the forensics, and when I repeated the information about the hotel's mailbox to Martin and Colin they were both furious, although it would be more accurate to say Martin was apoplectic with rage.

'How the bloody hell does that bloody woman manage to avoid bloody detection in every bloody thing she does?' he ranted. 'I could quite happily bloody well kill her my bloody self.'

'Has Louise upset you a tad Martin?' asked Sam with a broad grin on her face.

'Yes she bloody well has' he replied 'I just hate being defeated by anyone, especially when I don't know how they're doing it.' Then Martin started laughing. 'Sorry guys' he said 'It's just that I'm used to being on the winning side.'

'You still are on the winning side' said

Helena 'we just haven't reached the winning post yet. Come on folks, let's get down to that square and start asking a few pertinent questions.'

George was on 'watching' duty, and so Jo led us to the square, and once we got there we split up and started knocking on every door we could find. About ten minutes into the search Martin suddenly shouted:

'Got her. She's rented a room from this gentleman.'

We all joined Martin who was asking the grubby looking elderly concierge which room she'd rented. He was reluctant to help, but then Helena showed him her badge stating that she was the Head of Interpol's European Operations and she explained to him in fluent French that if he didn't want to spend the rest of his life in a French prison then he should start cooperating immediately. He generously did so and immediately offered her the key to room ten. Martin grabbed the key from Helena's outstretched hand and ran up the stairs to the first floor. Checking for basic simple security things like a hair across the door, which there wasn't, he let himself in. There was just a bed, a chair, a chest of drawers and a wardrobe in the room and a small rug alongside the bed. Martin was back out again five minutes later.

'Come on folks, let's get away from here before she finds us. This is definitely being used as her changing room. I'll fill you all in on the details when we get back.'

Back at our hotel Martin told us what he'd found.

'There was no paperwork anywhere, just a load of men's clothes hanging in the wardrobe and various theatrical bits and pieces, including a grey wig, a stick on moustache in one of the drawers, a pile of bandages and adhesive plaster and a box of theatrical make-up. What I found there matches exactly with the description of the old man that the chef's maid gave to the police. Louise must use it to get changed, go and do the job, go back there and get changed back into her own clothes and then stroll back to her hotel. I left the room exactly as I found it and she'll not know we've been there.'

'Unless the landlord tells her' suggested Sam

'Oh he won't say anything' said Martin smiling. 'I promised him that if we discovered he'd said a single solitary word to her, then I would return in the middle of the night and suspend him out of the top floor window by his genitals, using a length of rusty barbed wire. He'll keep quiet.'

'You can be really evil sometimes Martin.' said Sam laughing.

'Needs must as the saying goes' he commented shrugging his shoulders and smiling back at her.

'But there was definitely no sign of any drugs, syringes etc?' asked Sam.

'No, nothing at all' he answered. 'I assume Louise must keep all that sort of stuff somewhere else.' surmised Martin.

'Possibly somewhere in her hotel suite' I suggested.

'Sorry to disagree with you Michael' said Martin 'but if I was the poisoner the last place I'd keep any incriminating evidence is where I lived. I suspect she has two or three more of these seedy apartments tucked away all over Paris. Having dealt with that so called landlord earlier today we know that these type of men will rent a room to anyone, no questions asked for a few euros, and Louise can easily afford a hell of a lot of euros. We know she dressed as a female cleaner when she did the police HQ, but there were no women's clothes in that apartment, just the one man's outfit. So I'm pretty sure she must have other apartments somewhere.'

'God, that's really comforting to know.' said Colin.

'Then how the hell do we find them?' asked Jo.

'We continue doing what we're good at' said Helena 'well, most of the time we are good at it. We continue to follow her. Come on, let's go and relieve George, he's watching for Louise from the coffee shop on the other side of the road.

Chapter Twenty Five

Gemma's next and in her current thinking probably her final target was Baron Francois Leblanc, the owner of restaurant 'Seulement le meilleur'. The problem was there was no way of knowing when he was going to appear at the restaurant because he never knew himself. He just seemed to make up life as he went along. Secondly, and far more importantly, he didn't live in Paris.
Baron Francois Leblanc was sixty two years old, but still as fit as he was when he was thirty two. He ran at least three miles most mornings, he rode horses as well as any rodeo star, and he regularly indulged in his favourite hobby of

fencing, of which he once represented France at the Olympics. He was extremely wealthy and lived in a magnificent chateau in the Loire valley. The numerous châteaux of the Loire valley form a large part of the architectural history of the many towns stretched along the banks of the Loire River. These towns include Amboise, Blois, Chinon, Montsoreau, Nantes, Orléans, Saumur and Tours. There are over three hundred of these magnificent buildings in the Loire valley and they vary greatly in style from historic fortified castes to the magnificent houses and gardens simply designed to display the wealth of their owners.

Baron Francois Leblanc's château 'le Meilleur' fell into the latter category, and had been built to mimic the style of the far more illustrious the Château de Cheverny. The original building of 'Château de Cheverny' can be traced back to the early fourteenth century, although the present day version you see today was completely rebuilt between 1624 and 1630. Its main claim to fame is probably that of its elegant orangey, which was used during the Second World War as a secret safe haven from the Nazi's in which to hide many works of art brought down from the Louvre in Paris, including Leonardo da

Vinci's 'Mona Lisa.' Baron Francois Leblanc's 'Château le Meilleur' although many people dispute the authenticity of its title, is to all intents and purposes very similar in both style and age to 'de Cheverny', but in fact it only dates back to 1934 when his father, the previous Baron had had it built. So this was Gemma's final challenge. How to get her revenge on an incredibly fit man who lived in a fortified residence with highly trained and heavily armed security guards on the premises twenty four hours a day.

Gemma liked a challenge, and having got this far, there was now no rush.

Colin was watching for Louise, and the rest of us were in Helena's hotel bedroom.

'Surely it must be worth searching her hotel suite' I suggested. 'There's bound to be something in there that will help?'

'You need to understand Michael' answered Helena 'The way things are done in France is very different to the UK. For a start there is no such thing as a search warrant, and you can only enter a private property if people are in imminent danger. Now what that means in practice is for example if there has been a report of a gunshot, there is a fire taking hold, there is a fight taking place inside or a burglary in progress, perhaps the sound of people screaming from behind the door etc.

But even then, and if one of those incidents had been reported, it is only the National Police that have the authority to enter private premises, not Interpol. We would have to get Detective Chief Inspector Claude Moreau's permission and he would be in total charge and have to supervise everything we did.'

'Well we obviously can't allow that' I replied 'we'd have to tell the French Police everything we know.'

'If we did break in to Louise's hotel suite behind Claude Moreau's back' continued Helena 'and then got caught, you can imagine the outcry there would be in France, but bear in mind that is if we broke into private property. It would be ten times worse if Interpol got caught illegally breaking into one of Paris's top hotels. For a start we'd all get thrown out of Interpol and the French authorities would take great delight in prosecuting every one of us personally.'

'So I guess we're not breaking into Louise's hotel suite then' I said smiling.

'Well, never say never' said Helena smiling back. 'Martin's never been caught yet and I wouldn't expect him to be this time, particularly with the rest of us keeping watch and using delaying tactics while he made his escape, but for the moment, let's just continue following her.'

Gemma had been thinking long and hard about the problem and eventually decided there was no alternative but to go and see the château for herself. She telephoned the hotel's reception desk and informed them she would be away for a few days, but she would be back before the end of the week. Her hotel bill was paid weekly by a direct debit she had set up upon her arrival, so the hotel was not at all concerned about her running off anywhere. Gemma packed for a few days, which in Lady Louise mode meant two large suitcases, and a porter took them down to reception where they ordered her a taxi. Colin saw Lady Louise and her two large cases arrive in reception and immediately telephoned Helena from his mobile.

'Her ladyship's just arrived in reception with two large suitcases' reported Colin. 'God knows where she's off to, but it looks like she's ordered a taxi.'

'Get outside quick and grab a cab' ordered Helena. 'Don't let the cab driver know you are Interpol, he'll only blab about it later, pay cash and follow Louise wherever she goes. For all our sakes, don't lose her.'

Colin quickly ran outside and jumped into the first cab he saw. Fortunately the driver spoke excellent English as most French taxi drivers do if they want to cash in on the UK tourists. Colin was about to ask him to wait a moment when Louise and a porter arrived at the taxi in front. The porter instructed the driver to take Lady Louise to Paris Gare du Nord, the main railway station in the city. Colin had heard what the porter had said and offering the driver a large tip, instructed his own cab to get to the station as fast as possible so that he could be there when Louise arrived. He then relayed the information to Helena who informed him that everybody else would join him at the station as soon as possible. We all raced out of our own hotel and grabbed a couple of cabs to take us to Gare du Nord.

'You two will need to keep well out of sight' Helena said to Sam and I. 'She'll spot the pair of you a mile off and know immediately she's being followed. Likewise George with you and Jo. She may remember you from the square. We'll keep an eye on her and then let you know where she's off to and you guys can go and sort out some accommodation for us if necessary.

Again, don't let anyone know your Interpol, just book four twin rooms for a group of tourists and pay with the private Visa credit cards issued in your names but paid by Interpol.'

Having been promised a decent tip if he did so, Colin's cab managed to get him to Gare du Nord about two minutes before Louise arrived. Colin then hung around the ticket office to see if he could hear where she was going.

'Bonjour' Louise said to the ticket clerk when she got to the window. 'Parlez vous anglais s'il te plait' she said in about the only broken French she had learnt.

'Yes madam' he answered smiling 'fortunately for you I do.'

Colin had by this point managed to get himself into the queue standing immediately behind Louise.

'Excellent' Louise replied 'and thank you. Can I please have an open ended return ticket to Nantes'

'Certainly Madam' answered the ticket clerk. 'Do you know when you will be returning to Paris as that effects which ticket you purchase, today, later this week, a month?'

'Oh, I shall only be there a few days at most' said Louise. 'It is highly likely I will return to Paris at the end of the week.'

'Excellent madam. In that case that will be fourteen euros please, and the next train to Nantes leaves platform six in seventeen minutes.'

Colin, who was standing right behind Louise in the queue and had heard every word of their conversation, immediately purchased seven return tickets for the same destination once Louise was out of hearing range. He then telephoned Helena and told her they had just over ten minutes to get to the ticket barrier of platform six where he would be waiting for them. Louise had already gone on to the platform with a porter in tow carrying her suitcases, and Colin watched her walk virtually the entire length of the platform and enter the second carriage from the front.

We all made it to 'Gare du Nord' just in time, and we eventually settled down in the second carriage from the back.

'So' asked Helena. 'What on earth is she up to? Anyone got any ideas?'

'Perhaps she hates the people of Nantes as much as she hates the people of Paris, and she is going to murder nineteen of Nantes's poor citizens' I helpfully suggested.

'Thank you for your usual incredibly

helpful contribution Michael' said Helena sarcastically 'but personally I think she may have a specific target in mind, but heaven knows who.'

'Well this journey will take just over two hours' said Sam 'so I guess we've got just under two hours to search the internet and find out who lives in the area of Nantes and why Louise would be after them.'

We all got out our tablets and mobile phones and started trawling the internet for ideas, but two hours later we were none the wiser as the train pulled into Nantes.

'Remember to keep out of sight you four' instructed Helena. 'If she sees any of you all our covers will be blown. Colin, get up the front as fast as you can and keep an eye on her. Let us know where she's going, then once you know, let us know.'

Colin shot off and the rest of us walked down the platform and out into the heart of the station where we all grabbed a drink at the station coffee shop waiting on Colin's information. Colin was on the phone to Helena five minutes later.

'She's just taken a cab and is heading out into the countryside. I couldn't hear where she's going so I'm in a cab of my own and we appear to be heading to the south of the city.'

'OK Colin' said Helena. 'Thanks and please let me know when you get to wherever she's going.'

'Will do boss' replied Colin and he then hung up.

Fifteen minutes later Colin rang again.

'We've just entered the small town of Vertou and Louise's taxi has now stopped outside a guest house?

'Where exactly is Vertou' asked Helena?

'It's located to the south of Nantes on a small tributary of the main river that runs through Nantes.'

'OK Colin' said Helena 'just sit tight and we'll be there as soon as we can. I've hired a seven seater 4 x 4 and we're on our way.'

Louise had pre-booked herself into 'Les Sources de Cheverny' a top of the range hotel tucked away in its own private estate. The hotel's website had described it as the quintessential French château, exuding 18th-century elegance with the bygone grandeur with a homely charm. Now she had settled into her suite, she agreed.

Obviously we couldn't all risk staying in the same hotel as Louise, but we needed to be close, so Helena had booked myself, Sam, George, Jo and herself into the nearby 'Château de Troussay', while Colin and Martin, who were unknown to Louise, had got themselves a twin room at Louise's hotel 'Les Sources de Cheverny' where they would be on hand and could keep an eye on her Ladyship's movements.

Louise got changed into her 'Gemma' clothes as she felt she could think far clearer as 'Gemma' when she was dressed in jeans and a smart top, as opposed to being in 'Lady Louise' mode, dressed in beautiful dresses, gorgeous silks and fine fabrics.

Gemma knew she had been followed when she's spotted the man and woman in the square back in Paris, but she hadn't seen either of them since. However, that didn't mean she was in the clear and there was every possibility that she was still being followed even now. So, cunning was the order of the day. Gemma needed to get a good look at Baron Francois Leblanc's home, 'Château le Meilleur', but in order to throw anyone following her off the scent, she would also spend some time visiting one or two of the most famous Loire valley chateaux, and play the part of the typical English tourist. Her final choices were the incredible 'Chateau de Chambord' and the stunningly beautiful 'Chateau de Chenonceau'.

Her first choice was extremely obvious. Chateau de Chambord is a vast Renaissance extravagance started by the French King Francois I in the early 16th century as a hunting lodge. This vast and magnificent building contains over 400 rooms, 365 fireplaces and 84 staircases, and all this for a residence that was only used for 2 months during Francois's reign. He also created sumptuous hunting grounds, surrounded by an uninterrupted wall of 32km to contain his potential prey of deer and wild boar plus a stable for 1200 horses. The views of the external architecture and beyond from the roof terraces are breath-taking, and once when asked 'Why so much detail Francois?' he supposedly replied 'Because I could!'

Chateau de Chenonceau couldn't be more different, and it is the most visited and photographed chateau of the Loire Valley. It is often described as 'the ladies chateau' as throughout its history it is the ladies who have most influenced its design and its destiny. Thomas Bohier acquired what was a small fortress by the river Cher in 1512 and he decided to replace it with a new 'Renaissance' style chateau leaving only the keep from the original building. However it was his wife Katherine Briconnet who oversaw its design and build as her husband spent most of his time away at war, and she has left us all a great legacy. Henri II gave Chateau de Chenonceau to his mistress Diane de Poitiers, and it was she who added the bridge over the Cher as well as the gardens. When King Henri II died, the Queen, Catherine de Medici, forced Diane de Poitiers out of Chenonceau, and it was Catherine that built the gallery and grand ballroom on Diane's bridge which finally gave Chenonceau its now iconic look.

This 'throwing them off the scent' sight-seeing exercise Louise decided would take the next two days of her time, and hopefully it would either completely bore to death anyone following her, or if she was really lucky make them careless and she would spot them. Once she knew who they were she could hopefully lose them, and that would leave her in peace to study the Baron's 'Château le Meilleur'.

Chapter Twenty Six

Martin and Colin kept their distance from each other while they were inside the hotel 'Les Sources de Cheverny' or walking within the hotels grounds. The theory being that if Louise spotted one of them, the other could then take over. On the first morning Martin watched Louise during breakfast in the dining room, and then Colin took over when she arrived at the reception desk. He managed to get close enough to hear her order a taxi to take her to the Chateau de Chambord which she had heard so much about.

Colin rang Martin and suggested he get down to reception as soon as possible as her ladyship was about to leave. Martin had hired a small black Renault Clio for a few days the previous evening so that they wouldn't run the risk of losing her while waiting for a taxi to pick them up. Colin had the car keys with him and went and sat in the car with the engine running. Martin jumped in alongside him a minute later.

'Any idea where she's going?' asked Martin.

'Yes, some place called Chateau de Chambord' replied Colin 'wherever and whatever that is.'

'Good grief Colin' said a sarcastic Martin

'you really can be a total Philistine when you put your mind to it can't you?'

'I do my very best to live down to my reputation of being a thick Irishman' he said, then laughed. 'I gather it's the most over the top chateau in the whole of the Loire valley, possibly in all France, and apparently it even makes Versailles seem relatively normal.'

'Oh' said a startled Martin 'you have heard of it then.'

'It's not just you South Africans that do culture you know' laughed Colin.
At that point Louise appeared and climbed into the back of the waiting taxi. She glanced around as her taxi left to see if anyone was following her, but as Martin and Colin already knew where she was going, they just let her taxi disappear from sight before heading off after it.

Sitting in the back of her taxi, Louise was now fully in Gemma mode, both mind-set and dressed accordingly in black trousers and a smart zip fronted suede jacket. Gemma wasn't one hundred percent sure, but she had a very strong feeling that the man who was standing pretty close behind her at the hotel's reception desk that morning was the self-same man that had been standing behind her in the queue at

Gare do Nord. If it was, and thinking about it now she was more or less certain it was him, then it seemed to be highly likely that she was being followed. But who, or more importantly which organization would be following her? It was probably the DGSI, the Direction Générale de la Sécurité Intérieure, otherwise known as the General Directorate for Internal Security, France's equivalent of the UK's MI5, or maybe it was just the plain old French Police. Interpol never even crossed her mind.

But if all they were doing was simply following her, then that must mean they had no proof or they would have arrested her by now. Well, she reasoned to herself, how could they have proof? She'd worn latex gloves on every occasion therefore leaving no fingerprints, she'd always disposed of the syringes down drains or thrown them in the river, and whenever she'd been out and about getting her revenge on people, she'd always been dressed as someone other than herself, usually an elderly man or woman. So, what to do now? Gemma thought about it during the drive to Chateau de Chambord, and by the time they arrived she'd made her decision. She was in no great hurry to dispose of Baron Francois Leblanc, so whoever it was tailing her she'd simply bore them to death, or at least till they gave up following her every move.

'Bloody hell Martin' exclaimed Colin into his radio set 'is she going to wander around every bloody square inch of this damned chateau? My feet are absolutely bloody killing me. I think you need to take over before my feet start bleeding and we get thrown out for ruining their bloody marble floors.'

'Oh for goodness sake Colin' said a frustrated Martin 'is bloody the one and only adjective you know?'

'Oh, hold on Martin' Colin quickly replied cutting Martin's flow off 'it looks like she's heading for the chateau's exit. I'll see you back at the car.'

Colin followed Gemma back outside from about twenty to thirty feet behind her, and then once she was outside she jumped into one of the waiting taxi's. Martin arrived in the car park a few seconds later and once they were both on board, he and Colin shot off after the taxi. The taxi drove straight back to the hotel and apart from her evening meal in the hotel's restaurant, Gemma never left her suite all night.

The following day Gemma did exactly the same thing. She had breakfast, then got a taxi to

Chateau de Chenonceau where she spent six hours wandering around the chateau and the grounds taking several photographs en-route. Colin had been given the day off to let his feet recover, and Helena had gone on surveillance with Martin. What Helena and Martin hadn't realized was that on several occasions Gemma took photographs of reflections in windows as a means of seeing who was following her without having to look round behind her. Once she got back to the hotel Gemma uploaded all the photographs from her iPhone onto her laptop. She zoomed in on the reflected faces, used some computer software to clean up the pictures and she now had glorious full colour photographs of Martin, Helena and Colin who she had managed to photograph using the same devious method the previous day. That evening Gemma phoned down to reception and extended her booking at the hotel for another seven days. One thing was for sure, the Loire Valley was not short of chateau's to visit, and Gemma was sure she would drive whoever it was that was following her mad, by doing absolutely nothing wrong and so for the next week she would simply behave like a boring English tourist. Which is exactly what she did.

'She must be on to us' I said. 'She has to be, nobody is that enthralled with visiting one chateau after another like this. She's just winding us up.'

'I suspect' said Colin agreeing 'that she's recognized me from being up close to her at both the railway station ticket office in Paris and then again in the queue for reception at the hotel.'

'She's been taking photographs like mad wherever she's been' said Martin 'and I bet she's got pictures of all of us from our reflections in windows. I thought yesterday that she was taking lots of photos of windows for no apparent reason and then I realized last night why. I should have known, I've done exactly the same thing myself often enough.'

'So she knows what Michael and Sam look like' said Helena 'as she knows both of them reasonably well. We're pretty sure she'd recognize Jo and George from the square in Paris, and now we're pretty sure she's got pictures of Colin, Martin and myself. There is now nobody here who can follow her without being spotted. I'm going to call Amsterdam and get my top surveillance team of eight on the next flight to Paris. They can take over surveillance duties from now on and leave the rest of us free to do some investigative work.'

Helena did so, and the eight Interpol operatives having caught the first flight they could out of Schiphol arrived at our hotel just before midnight. They all checked in just before we checked out. They were a right mixed bunch to look at, and not one of them looked like they'd even be granted an interview with Interpol, never mind be the best 'watchers' in the business as the Brits called them. There was a young loved up Indian couple, an elderly spinster, three middle aged white men, a Jamaican born guy in his early twenties and a young Chinese woman. In fact they were all Dutch nationals, and all eight of them spoke fluent Dutch, English and French. Helena had recruited each one of them herself and they were all brilliant at what they did. We all met with the eight newcomers for a thorough briefing, all squashed into one of our bedrooms and having been told everything they needed to know by Helena about Lady Louise/Gemma, the rest of us left and headed back to Paris one of the night trains. Colin and Martin having been telephoned by Helena had also checked out and they met us at the station having left the hire car in the station car park. We got back to Paris around four in the morning and all went to our own beds.

Chapter Twenty Seven.

The following morning we all met for a late breakfast in our own hotel's restaurant. The surveillance team were busy following Lady Louise who was visiting yet another chateau, and so far she had apparently done nothing other than take photographs and act the part of the perfect tourist. After breakfast we all went up to Helena's room which we were using as our conference room.

'Look, we know she is playing tourist in the Loire Valley, so why don't we use this opportunity of her being away to go through her hotel suite?' I asked:

'Too dangerous and too soon' answered Helena. 'Firstly, it's dangerous for us because her suite will be being watched as the hotel staff know she is away for a few days, and if you remember Sam, she told you she has a lot of valuable jewellery in her room safe, which she's more than likely told the staff as well.'

'Yes, you're right, she did' replied Sam.

'Secondly, continued Helena 'we'll only get the chance to search her room once and I'd rather wait until we've got a better idea of where to look and more to the point what to look for.'

'So what do we do then?' asked George.

'We look for any other apartments that she may be using. We know about the one in the square where she keeps the elderly man outfit, but we also know she has dressed and played the part of an elderly woman when she visited Le Figaro's reception to drop off the first letter. She wouldn't have gone all the way to the newspapers offices dressed as the old woman, so she must have somewhere near where she got changed. Let's spread out in the area around Le Figaro and see if we can find that apartment. Knock on every door, find the concierges or the apartment managers, show them the photographs you've got of Louise and telephone me if you find it. Then we'll all head there and decide what to do next together.'

We all headed off towards Le Figaro's offices. Sam and I took one side of the road and searched for apartments to the east of Le Figaro, while Helena and Martin searched west of their offices. On the other side of the road Colin, George and Jo searched individually knocking on any and every apartment door they could find.

Our instructions from Helena had been very clear.

'When you find a concierge or a manager,

don't say you're from Interpol or show them your warrant cards or badges. You are looking for your sister who sent you a message to meet up with her this afternoon, but somehow you've stupidly lost the address and you wondered if she had rented a room in this block. If you should get a yes, then show them your Interpol authority and keep them with you until the rest of us get there.'

It took over one and a half hours before we had any success, and then Jo telephoned Helena.

'The concierge of this pretty run down block of apartments says he thought the woman who had rented the apartment looked like my sister, but he'd only seen her once when she paid him a couple of months' rent in advance, in cash obviously.'

Jo gave Helena directions to the apartment block over the phone, and then Helena radioed us all with the directions and told us all to head there straight away. Helena and Martin were actually the last two to arrive and Martin took the key from the very grubby looking concierge who appeared not to have washed for days, and then headed up to the room. Martin asked me to accompany him as we'd done this sort of search together on numerous other occasions, and I was familiar with his methods and more importantly his rules. Martin checked the outside for basic warnings like a hair stuck across the door and the door frame, but there was nothing. Martin unlocked the door and we went inside. We knew immediately we'd found the right apartment. Martin examined the door of the wardrobe and found a black hair across the door and the frame. He carefully noted its position and then removed it putting it inside the bedside cabinet drawer. He then opened the wardrobe and inside found not only the old ladies outfit, but a set of pretty grubby cleaner's overalls.

'I think we've hit pay dirt my friend' said Martin. 'These must be the overalls she wore when she did the police HQ dressed as a cleaner, and I guess these are the props she used.' Martin was pointing at a bucket sitting on the floor of the wardrobe with a brush, a couple of dusters and a plastic sandwich box sitting inside it. Martin carefully noted the position of the sandwich box and then removed it.

'I really can't imagine she used this for a packed lunch' said Martin 'nobody in their right mind takes a packed lunch with them on a murder expedition, so let's see what the hell she did use it for.'
Martin carefully lifted the lid off the box and

inside he found a white cardboard box. Inside the box he found three unused syringes wrapped in foam rubber. The three syringes were all empty. Martin replaced the syringes and foam rubber in the box exactly as he'd found them and then turned the box over. On the other side was an address label from an internet firm based in Bulgaria. The label was addressed to Madame Genevieve Ballenger, and the address was a post office box not far from the apartment.

'My guess.' said Martin 'is that she orders the strychnine, thallium etc from this dodgy internet firm in Bulgaria, and has it delivered to a PO Box she has opened in the name of this Madame Genevieve Ballenger.'

'This is unusually careless of her to leave this stuff just sitting in a wardrobe' I said, but Martin came straight back at me.

'She has to keep it all somewhere, and as far as she knows, nobody has the vaguest idea she uses this place. There is no paperwork trail, she has only met the concierge once when she paid him in cash, plus she would simply deny it was her if she was ever accused and she can't keep anything incriminating in the hotel suite. Come on, let's put everything back exactly as we found it and get out of here.'

Martin replaced everything including the hair

across the door of the wardrobe, locked the front door and we headed back downstairs to the rest of the team.

Chapter Twenty Eight.

Gemma was enjoying herself immensely in the Loire Valley. She hadn't seen any of the usual followers from Paris, and she assumed they had all been replaced with a selection of fresh faces. What the hell she thought, I'm doing absolutely nothing wrong so whoever is watching me can do so to their hearts content. She would drive them mad with boredom. Over the next week she visited Château du Clos Lucé, Château d'Ussé, Château d'Azay-le-Rideau, Château d'Amboise and on her last day Château de Langeais. She thought she might have spotted one or two possible followers, but then again it may have been people just doing what she was doing, touring the best chateaux in the Loire Valley.

Maurice Rossiter, the leader of the surveillance team reported in to Helena every morning and every evening, but he had absolutely nothing to report other than they'd had yet another nice day viewing a bloody French Château.

'Without a doubt she knows we're on to her' said Martin. 'She's now decided to just play with us.'

'I agree' I said 'Louise must have spotted one or two of us over the last couple of weeks and realized she was under surveillance, so she's just doing nothing in the hope we'll get bored and call it a day.'

'What do we actually have on her?' asked Sam.

'That's the annoying thing' replied Helena. 'We know for sure that Lady Louise Hamilton Smythe and Mrs Gemma Louise Borgert are one and the same person, but we have no actual proof. We know she is the poisoner of nineteen French citizens, but again, we don't have a scrap of evidence or proof. We know she has rented two apartments where she gets changed into various disguises, but nothing is in her name and again there is no proof. I've checked out the PO Box she used in the name of Madame Genevieve Ballenger, but it was a cash transaction for just three months. Again there is absolutely nothing linking it to Louise and for all we know she may have three other apartments and four more PO Boxes.'

'If she's sensible' said Martin 'and I believe she is not only very sensible crime wise, but also extremely intelligent, then she won't go back to anywhere she's been before. I think we could stake out both of those apartments twenty four hours a day every day of the week for the next year, and she won't go anywhere near them.'

'How about getting DNA from the clothing she's left at the two apartments and comparing it with Louise's DNA?' I asked.

'No point' said Martin. 'Tell me Michael, did you smell anything in that wardrobe?'

'Yeees' I replied slowly. 'Thinking about it, I did. There was a slight smell of bleach or something similar, but I didn't think anything of it. Why?'

'If you want to remove your DNA from fabrics' replied Martin 'you wash them in a bleaching agent. You could use 96% ethanol which will remove all traces of amplifiable DNA by 100 to 200 times, or even better you the clean clothes with hypochlorite to remove all traces of amplifiable DNA. The giveaway that makes me certain that is what she's done is the smell of bleach.'

'God, she thinks of everything' mused Sam.

'I did say she's extremely intelligent' said Martin smiling at Sam.

'Look I don't think there's any point in keeping our best surveillance team tied up here in France any longer when there's much better things for them to be doing elsewhere. I'm calling them off as soon as Louise returns to Paris. I'm sure between us we can keep an eye on her, even if it is from a distance. We'll start tomorrow once she's up and about.'
Which she did, arriving around noon the following day.

Louise telephoned Sam from her suite at the Four Seasons virtually the minute she got back, and invited us both over for afternoon tea. We readily accepted and duly arrived at 3.30 pm.
'Oh you two would have absolutely loved the Loire Valley' she began to tell us excitedly. 'I found it really interesting, and if only you could have been there and seen all the amazing places I saw and the many interesting people I spotted.'
She obviously knew full well that we had been there, and that we did see all the places she saw, and it was her way of saying that as well as spotting us at some point, she'd also seen all the 'interesting' people following her, but without actually saying so or admitting anything.
If she had somehow seen us, she would now know the people following her were from

Interpol, and therefore that Sam and I were on to her. But at this stage she obviously wanted to play games with us, so for the moment we played along. I was interested to find out what she was planning next.

'So what's next Louise?' I asked 'more chateaux visits, or how about a few French vineyards. I gather they know how to make decent wine in this country.'

'Well I definitely know how to drink it' she laughed. 'Actually Michael that might be a really good idea. Mmm, a few vineyard trips, fancy joining me you two?

'Sorry, we can't' said Sam 'as much as we'd like too, but we've still got this wretched Mrs Borgert to find.'

'Oh yes, of course' came back Louise. 'Having any joy on that front?'

'Well we've got quite a few ideas and several leads' said Sam 'but as you can imagine it's obviously all very hush hush and confidential.'

'Of course' Louise retorted 'I understand. I wouldn't dream of asking you to break your oaths and share any confidentialities.'
Like hell you wouldn't I thought.

'So when do you think you might head off again?' asked Sam.

'Well as much as I adore Paris and love the people here, there is so much more of France to see, and that was a great idea of Michael's. I think I might hire a car and visit a few vineyards over the next week or so.'

'And then you'll come back here again to the Four Season's?' asked Sam.

'Oh yes, most certainly' Louise came back quickly 'I certainly haven't finished achieving everything I want to in Paris.'
I bet you haven't I thought. But this ridiculous conversation was getting us nowhere and Louise was now just winding us up by deliberately playing little miss innocent. If we didn't leave I'd probably hit her. So we made our excuses and left.

Louise went to bed early at 7.30 pm and set her alarm for 2.30 am. By 3.00 am she was showered and changed into jeans, a white polo necked jumper and her maroon zip fronted suede jacket. She also wore a pair of white trainers on her feet as she thought they would be the most sensible footwear for the task ahead. She had packed a bag and then very quietly and discreetly she made her way down the emergency exit stairs at the end of her corridor. She saw nobody and more importantly, nobody saw her leaving the hotel. Now in 'Gemma' mode she walked to the nearest railway station where she had asked the car rental company to leave a Renault Koleos she had paid for in full with one of her credit cards. She wasn't in the least bit bothered that the police or Interpol might trace her through the car and her credit card, because in her mind even if they did, it would all be far too late by then.

Gemma drove through the night and eventually arrived in the town of Saumur in the Loire Valley just before 7.00 am. She had already booked into the Hotel Chateau de Verrieres and Spa by telephone, and having warned them of her expected arrival time, the reception desk were expecting her and had her room ready and waiting. Gemma went straight upstairs, locked the door and slept solidly for three hours. The alarm she'd set woke her and feeling greatly refreshed, Gemma got into the hire car and drove to the property of Baron Francois Leblanc, the Château 'le Meilleur'. Having arrived outside the entrance gates she didn't stop, but just drove round the outer walls looking for a possible entry point. Having completed a full circuit around the grounds of the property she set off again and this time she slowed right down when she reached a wooded area on the southern side of the grounds. Gemma pulled the car off the road and got out. She then clambered up the outside of the eight foot high stone wall and peered over the top. She couldn't see any security cameras, patrolling guards, trip wires or anything else that might set off alarms, and so she lowered herself down again and made an entry in the small notebook she had taken with her of exactly where this possible entry point was located. Gemma then got back in the car and slowly drove on again looking for more possible entry points. An hour later Gemma drove back to the hotel having now located four possible ways onto the grounds, hopefully without being detected.

She would return later in the day, once it was dark.

Chapter Twenty Nine.

Sam and I joined the rest of the team in Helena's bedroom and we sat down to plan our next move. Jo was watching Louise's room, but as yet there's been no sign of her.

'So what now O glorious leader?' asked Colin.

'I think the time has come for Martin to have a look inside her hotel suite' replied

Helena. 'It may be risky, but now she knows we're on to her she'll just be on her best behaviour and try and bore us to death.'

'Do we know where she is at the moment?' I asked.

'I assume she's still in her hotel suite' answered Helena 'Jo will let us know as soon as Louise appears, but why don't you give her a ring on her mobile and see if she'll meet you two for a coffee somewhere?'

I rang Louise's mobile straight away and she answered after the third ring.

'Good morning Michael' she said chirpily, 'and I trust you and Sam are both well this lovely day?'

'Yes, we're both fine thank you.' I replied

'Well I'm doing just what you suggested. I'm off looking at vineyards and doing some wine tasting over the next few days.'

'Oh great' I answered. 'When do you leave and can we meet up with you for coffee first and wish you bon voyage?'

'Oh, that would have been nice Michael, but as it happens I couldn't sleep last night, so I got up and left hours ago. I'm hoping to reach Chateau Latour by midday. My sat nav in the car says it's near Pauillac in the Medoc region of Bordeaux, so it should be wonderful scenery.

Let's have a good catch up when I get back. Look, I'm sorry to cut you off Michael, but I must go, the traffic here is really heavy and I need to concentrate. The last thing we need is for me to have an accident and then end up killing someone. Bye.'

And with that the line went dead.

'She's well and truly screwed us' I reported to everyone. 'She obviously sneaked out in the middle of the night and has headed off somewhere in a hire car.'

'Did she say where she was going?' asked George.

'Yes, she claims she's on her way to Pauillac in the Medoc region of Bordeaux, which means she's probably headed in the exact opposite direction.'

'Well it appears that we've lost her for the time being' mused Helena 'and if she's left Paris I assume she's not going to be killing anyone today as all her killings and targets are Parisian residents.'

'Maybe she's going after someone with a connection to Paris and her revenge vendetta, but they actually live somewhere else?' suggested Sam.

'Mmm, could well be' said Helena. 'Look, let's stop speculating and do something positive.

I'll get Jo back straight away, and now we know she'll be away for several hours at least, so Martin, can you let yourself into her suite and search it from top to bottom. Do you want anyone inside with you to help?'

'Yes' answered Martin 'it would be really useful if Michael came in with me. We've done this sort of thing several times together now and he knows my routines and more importantly, he knows and follows my rules.'

'Fair enough' said Helena. 'The rest of us will form a protective shield around you both. We'll use a radio link between Martin and myself and we'll position two of our people at both ends of the corridor. If anyone staff or cleaners etc approaches, delay them while I radio Martin and get him and Michael out of the suite. So, Martin and Michael will get themselves inside the suite, George and Jo will go the south end of the corridor and while Colin and Sam take the north end. I'll hover outside the door of the suite and keep in constant touch with Martin. Fortunately for us there are no CCTV cameras on any of the corridors. Any questions anyone?'

There wasn't, and so we headed off to the Four Seasons.

Once we'd arrived, being careful to do so in dribs and drabs so as not to look like an invading gang, everyone took up their positions as Helena had outlined earlier, and once she'd given us the all clear, Martin started work on the hotel suites door lock. He'd brought his usual four silver cases containing all his various burgling gadgets with him, and we were inside the suite within a minute. Helena had found a seat near Louise's hotel suite door and she at herself down. If any staff member enquired she would simply say she was feeling a little faint and needed to rest a moment.

'OK Michael' began Martin once we were inside. 'I'll take the lounge, you start in the bedroom.'
We opened bedroom drawers, went through wardrobes, looked in cupboards and on desktops etc, but we found nothing.

'Michael' said Martin quietly 'can you please bring me the silver case with the red dot near the handle.'
Martin had brought four silver briefcases with him as he always did on these kind of jobs, and between them they contained everything he ever needed. Each case had a different coloured dot near the cases handle, one red, one blue, one green and one yellow. I took him the case with

the red dot over to him and he placed it on the end of the bed alongside himself and opened it. Martin was looking to get into the room safe in Louise's bedroom and like most problems he came across, he had a gadget for solving whatever the problem was. Fortunately the room safe in Louise's hotel suite was nothing special, just the usual room safe you will find in most hotel rooms around the world. A strong metallic box attached to the wall inside one of the bedroom wardrobes, with a pad to one side on which you punch in your own secret four digit code. Martin took out of the silver case a small black box about six inches by four inches and two inches deep. On the front of the box were four push buttons, a small liquid crystal display, an on/off switch and a small red light. The back of the small gadget was magnetic and Martin carefully attached it to the front of the room safe, near its keypad where you punch in your own private code.

He turned the device on illuminating the small red light to show it was working, and then he pressed the button furthest to the left of the four. The display did nothing for a minute or so, and then it suddenly showed the number 7 on the far left hand side of the display. Martin then pressed the second button from the left and a minute or so later the digit 3 appeared after the 7. Having completed the same action on all four buttons the display now read 7345. Martin pulled the black box off of the room safe and returned it to its silver case, and then he punched 7345 into the room safes keypad. There was quick whirring sound, and a second later the room safes door popped slightly open.

Martin looked carefully inside the room safe through the small opening he now had using a torch he'd got from the same silver case.

'I don't expect to find a booby trap inside' he told me smiling 'but it's far better to be safe than sorry, if you'll excuse the pun.'

I just smiled. Martin then pulled the door fully open.

'Well, well, well' he commented 'I do believe I am looking at half a dozen syringes full of some liquid or other. I can only assume at this stage its Louise's last remaining stock of strychnine.'

'Do we take it or leave it?' I asked.

'Better check with the boss' he answered. 'There's also a small notebook here.'

Martin pulled out the thick notebook which turned out to be a page a day diary. He handed it to me and I started scanning through the pages.

'My God' I said startled 'Louise has written down everything she's been thinking as well as everything she's done. From what I can see with a quick glance, she mentions every murder, and why in her mind these people deserved to die. This is the evidence we've been waiting for.'

'Er, I'm afraid not' said Martin. 'The syringes and the diary were obtained by an illegal search, and any decent lawyer in the country would have both the syringes and the diary made inadmissible as evidence.'

'So what do we do?' I asked

'As I said before' answered Martin 'let's ask the boss.'

Martin got on the radio to Helena who was still sitting outside the hotel suite, and explained exactly what we had found and she immediately said we should take both the syringes and the diary.

'We'll worry about all the legal problems when and if this should ever get to court' explained Helena. 'We simply can't leave half a dozen syringes of strychnine laying around waiting for someone else to be killed by this maniac. Bring the diary as well, and I suggest you get out of there as soon as possible.'

Martin and I repacked the safe cracking gadget

and the torch inside the silver case, and carrying all four cases between us we left Louise's hotel suite the second Helena gave us the all clear, and then we all left the Four Seasons and headed back to our own hotel.

Chapter Thirty

Gemma had slept for a few hours and then went shopping in the afternoon. Most people go shopping for life's essentials, food, clothes, pills and various potions to cure colds and flu etc, but not Gemma. Once Gemma had decided that the Baron was going to be her final moment of revenge, she'd did a massive amount o0f research online. Then it was simply a matter of making numerous phone calls until she found someone who stocked exactly what she needed. Gemma found what she wanted in a sports shop in the town of Poitiers, a ninety minute drive south of Saumur. Having already checked by telephone that they had everything in stock she set off for the shop, Gemma only had to arrive, collect what she'd ordered and pay the large bill, which she did in cash she had previously withdrawn through the ATM system back in Paris before she left. The shop's proprietor showed Gemma the goods she'd ordered, gave her a quick crash course on the best way to use the equipment, and bade her farewell. Gemma arrived back at the hotel in time for an early supper.

What Gemma had purchased was in fact a 'Tenpoint Turbo Gt', a sporting crossbow specifically designed for large game hunting. She'd chosen this particular crossbow for several reasons. Firstly the 360 feet per second speed puts it right at the top of crossbows that can take down big game. Secondly a wide range of accessories is supplied with the crossbow including a high power scope, arrows, and a quiver.

Lastly, it had something called an integrated rope cocker which the store manager explained to her keeps the draw weight at a minimum and therefore makes using the crossbow more convenient. The scope, something called a 3X Pro-View 2 scope was really pleasing as it greatly enhanced the capabilities of the crossbow itself. It had crisp and bright optics, but most importantly for Gemma's purposes the scope came with an illuminated red/green reticule that would aid her when shooting at a target in less than ideal light conditions. Gemma didn't want to just kill the baron, she wanted him to suffer, but she knew he was a very fit man and in a one to one situation, she was far from confident that she would come out on top. So, she needed to get the poison into him, but it had to be from a distance. Watching a Discovery channel TV documentary a few nights earlier she had been fascinated in how the natives in South America had used poison tipped darts and blowpipes against the early Christian missionaries, and then there were the early Chinese who used poison tipped arrows in archery bows.

It set her thinking, and Gemma knew a full length long bow was out of the question, but a crossbow might just work for her. She went on line and searched the internet and decided the technology of the modern sporting crossbows could more than compensate for her lack of skill. Gemma even came across an article on the internet quoting a 17th-century account describing how arrow poisons were prepared in China. It read, 'The chosen liquid poison, being highly viscous and poisonous, is smeared on the sharp edges of arrowheads. These treated arrowheads are effective in the quick killing of both human beings and animals, even though the victim may shed only a slight trace of blood.' That short article was more than enough for

Gemma, and after all, she didn't want to kill the Baron with the crossbow, that would be far too easy a death for him. No, like his chef, the now deceased Raphael D'Aurevilly who the Baron had continued to employ despite him having killed poor Matthias, she wanted him to suffer the full experience of strychnine poisoning. So all that was needed was a harmless shot into his arm, or his thigh, in fact anywhere on his body that wouldn't bring about his immediate death and then she'd let the strychnine do the rest. Achieving that simple task shouldn't be too hard.

We'd all returned to our own hotel and gathered in Helena's room as usual. I say room, it was in fact a suite. Helena always booked a suite for herself when on a job, she said it was so that the team always had somewhere to meet where we could discuss everything in relative comfort, but let's be honest, suites were much nicer than rooms, she was the boss and after all Interpol were paying!

'I've read through all of Louise's diary entries' began Helena 'and they make pretty scary reading. I do understand how distressed the death of her husband has made her, and the fact that nobody was ever punished for it, not the chef, not the restaurant owner, not the attending doctor, but it still doesn't excuse in any way shape or form her killing of nineteen people, most of whom were totally innocent and knew absolutely nothing of the original poisoning of her husband, which was I'm sure totally accidental.'

'Does she show any regret for what she's done?' asked Sam.

'No, none whatsoever' replied Helena 'and that's the most worrying thing about everything she's written. She talks in the diary about how she feels she is now two completely different people, Lady Louise who is totally carefree and enjoying life and who has nothing to do with the killings, and Mrs Gemma Borgert, who has no aims in life other than revenging her husband's death. As far as we know she's still out there somewhere planning even more killings. We have no choice now, we have to get her off the streets and locked up, evidence or no evidence.'

'The main problem seems to be finding her' said George. 'I know she said she was off looking at vineyards in the Medoc region of Bordeaux for a few days, but as Michael said, that probably means she's driven off in the opposite direction.'

'A thought occurs to me' I said.

'Steady on dear' said Sam 'you had one of those last year and then you were trying to recover from it for weeks after.'

'Please ignore my wife' I requested.

'Sorry dear' said Sam giggling 'I love you really'.

'Mmm, yes well' I mused 'for some unknown reason I still love you.'
Everyone smiled.

'Now' I continued 'my thought is actually about something Helena said just now. If I remember rightly you said 'nobody was ever punished for it, not the chef, not the restaurant owner, not the attending doctor.'

'Yes, that's right' confirmed Helena.

'Well' I said thinking aloud 'Mrs Borgert has certainly punished the chef and the attending doctor by poisoning them both with strychnine, but as far as we know, she hasn't killed the restaurant owner, whoever that is. I assume it must be quite a strong possibility that she's gone after him or her, and if she's not got to them yet then the very least we can do is warn them.'

'Do we have any idea who owns the restaurant?' asked Jo.

'Haven't a clue' I replied.

'I'll check on the internet' said Martin who turned on the Interpol laptop that was sitting on the desk in the lounge area of Helena's suite, and started searching.

'There's no mention of the owner on the restaurant's website' said Martin 'just the names of the Executive Chef and the Maitre D. We can't even go and ask who the owner is at the restaurant because it's currently closed due to a bereavement.'

'I wonder who's died?' asked Colin. We all just looked at him.

'Sorry guys, wasn't thinking' he said smiling and then he shrugged.

'Detective Chief Inspector Claude Moreau will probably know who owns the restaurant' said Jo 'and if he doesn't he can probably find out.'

'True' responded Helena 'but then he'll want to know why we are asking and the last thing we need at this stage is the Paris police interfering.'

'Well whoever it is' I said 'it's a fair bet that they don't live in Paris, otherwise Louise wouldn't be driving somewhere round the French countryside.'

'Agreed' said Helena 'but firstly we need to know exactly where in the French countryside she's gone.'

Helena thought for a moment, then said

'George, can you and Martin please go and pop into a couple of the local posh restaurants and ask them if there is some sort of official register kept somewhere that lists the owners of restaurants in Paris.'

'We have the Chamber of Commerce in the UK' said Sam 'perhaps they have something similar here.'

'That may well be the case' replied Helena 'but I'm pretty sure membership is optional, and if you don't want people to know you own something then you don't join, or you list it in someone else's name.'

'Louise must have found out somehow' said Colin.

George and Martin left together, then split up when they reached the hotel lobby. George turned to the right and Martin turned to the left. They were both back within ten minutes.

'We're in luck' said Martin. 'The sous chef in the second restaurant I went in knew who owned 'Seulement le meilleur' as he'd once applied for a job there. He said the head chef liked him and was prepared to take him on, but the owner, and I quote 'who is a pompous arse called Baron Francois Leblanc said he didn't think he would fit in with the elegant ambiance of the restaurant and the class of superior clientele he was trying to attract.'

'Did he know where this Baron Leblanc lives?' asked Helena.

'No, afraid not' replied Martin 'but he said he thought the Baron owned some posh castle like building in the Loire valley.'

'So that's why Louise was traipsing round the Loire valley.' I said thinking aloud. 'She wasn't on a cultural jolly, she was surveying the home of her next target.'

George had gone over to the laptop and put in the name of Baron Francois Leblanc. There was a Wikipedia entry listing him as the current owner of a pretentious copy of the famous 'Château de Cheverny' built by his father, the fourteenth Baron. Apart from that there was no mention of an actual address, although there was reference to his sporting prowess and Olympic Games contributions. George then continued his search by putting in 'Château de Cheverny' and he quickly found a small sub entry stating that the building had been copied almost brick for brick by the fourteenth Baron Leblanc who had built it as a home for himself and his family. The article finished by saying it was apparently called 'Château le Meilleur' and it was located near the town of Saumur. George relayed all this information to everybody else and Helena immediately instructed us all to jump in the two cars we had hired and head for Saumur straight away.

Chapter Thirty One

Gemma had found a spot in the surrounding wall where she could climb over and hide amongst the many trees and thick undergrowth. This area of the estate was more or less left to grow wild, and it suited her needs perfectly. She had taken the crossbow with her along with three crossbow arrows, or bolts as the shop owner had explained they were called, and two vials of strychnine. Gemma had purchased a pack of twelve additional identical bolts to practice with, and as always wearing a pair of tight fitting transparent latex gloves, and having found a quiet area of woodland she had enjoyed aiming at tree trunks from 50 yards, and after two failed attempts she had finally hit the trunk she was aiming for with her third shot. She walked over to a thicker tree trunk and pinned to the tree one of numerous twelve inch square coloured bullseyes she had also purchased at the sports shop. After three attempts she managed to hit the target, although nowhere near the centre. She shot three more bolts and having got all three somewhere within the confines of the bulls eye, she retrieved all the bolts she had shot using a pair of strong pliers, and then she'd taken down the bullseye. Gemma was now positive that if she could hit a small target from fifty yards, then she could certainly hit a man, even if he was riding a horse.

Gemma enquired at a local shop in the town if the Baron needed any staff, cleaners, maids etc and the shopkeeper had helpfully suggested Gemma speak to Madam Boutons, who lived four doors down the road. He knew she regularly did some cleaning for the Baron, and she would probably know about any possible vacancies. Gemma knocked on her door and in a really friendly chatty way Gemma discovered during the conversation that the Baron usually went riding around the estate most lunchtimes, usually following a route that took him through the wooded area she was now waiting in. She that had been nearly two hours ago and now looking at her watch it was approaching twelve thirty, but there was no sign of him. Gemma had taken three of the crossbows bolts and carefully unscrewing the cap of the strychnine vials she had dipped the tips of all three bolts into the poison. One of the bolts was in the crossbow waiting for the Baron to appear, and the other two bolts were laying alongside her on top of the grass undergrowth. Gemma, wearing a dark green cotton jumper and black jeans was well hidden behind a large bush, but she could clearly see any rider that might be approaching. Half an hour later Gemma heard a church bell somewhere indicating it was now one o'clock, and just as she was beginning to despair she saw two riders on horses approaching. She hadn't bargained on their being two riders, but she immediately made up her mind the other rider would have to go as well. The Baron was easily recognisable with his neat silver hair, and sitting astride a magnificent grey stallion, the other rider was a woman she estimated to be at least twenty years younger than the Baron, riding a smaller chestnut horse, but a twenty year age difference was not unusual in the world of very wealthy men.

Taking careful aim, Gemma fired the first bolt aiming for the Baron's chest. With another rider along she was not prepared to risk trying a fancy shot, so she decided to aim for the biggest target she could see. Unfortunately, or from Gemma's point of view fortunately, being very inexperienced in the world of crossbows she had not made allowances for the horse's forward movement, so the bolt hit the Baron slightly behind where she had aimed and hit him fair and square in the bicep of his right arm. The Baron clutched his arm and fell from his horse which then bolted. His female companion had heard and seen nothing of the crossbow bolt and didn't realize the Baron had been shot and she stopped her horse and dismounting simply cried aloud,

'Oh Francois, are you OK?'

Gemma meanwhile, still hiding unseen behind the bush, had now reloaded the crossbow with a second bolt, and was now aiming it at the woman. The woman heard the bush rustle as Gemma stood to take aim, and just as she was about to ask what was going on a strychnine tipped bolt landed in the centre of her chest. She was dead long before the strychnine took any effect.

Gemma left the cover of the bush and walked over to the baron who was now starting to feel the effects of the strychnine. Gemma said nothing, but just stood there watching the agony start to work its way through his entire body.

She had no desire to be caught, so she simply collected the two bolts pulling them out of the bodies, picked up the crossbow and spare bolts and headed back to the wall where she had originally entered the estate. She clambered back over the wall, threw the crossbow and spare bolts in the boot of the car and then drove back to the Hotel Chateau de Verrieres and Spa as fast as possible. When she got back to the hotel Gemma left the crossbow and the bolts locked in the boot of the hire car, ran up the stairs to her room, collected all her belongings and after paying the bill she drove away, not really knowing where she was going, as long as it was a long way from the 'Château le Meilleur'.

We arrived at 'Château le Meilleur' to find the local police blocking the entrance. George, who spoke excellent French volunteered to go and ask the gendarme if there was a problem. On his return to the car George informed us that it looked like we had sadly arrived too late. He informed us that Mrs Borgert had most definitely struck again. We raced back to Paris in the hope of catching and arresting Louise back at the Four Seasons, but by the time we arrived, she had beaten us to it by an hour. She had collected all her luggage, paid her bill, closed her account, returned her keys and checked out, this time for good.

Gemma had left the Baron's 'Château le Meilleur' in a bit of a daze. She wasn't at all sure where she was going, but she knew she needed to collect her belongings from the Four Seasons. Upon getting back to Paris, entering her hotel suite and opening the room safe in her bedroom, she realized immediately that she had been rumbled and would probably be arrested soon, so the most important thing was to get away as fast as possible. This she did, leaving with all her luggage by the rear entrance, dropping her keys in a key box and then paying her final bill and checking out for good with a brief telephone call. Gemma then drove south heading towards Cannes on the French Riviera, a town and area she knew well. She knew she needed to get rid of the crossbow and bolts as soon as possible, but she also needed to do so a long way from Paris. Looking at the GPS on her hire car she knew that even if she drove non-stop she wouldn't get to Cannes until the early hours as Paris to Cannes by road was about an eight and half hour journey. Gemma arrived in the city of Auxerre in the late evening just as dusk was settling over the town, and she decided she would overnight here and go on to Cannes in the morning. Gemma checked into a fairly nondescript hotel, had a meal and then grabbed a few hours' sleep lying fully clothed on the bed. At 2.00 am her alarm went off and Gemma quietly descended the staircase of the hotel and went out to the hotel's car park where she had left the hire car. She had backed it up against a high brick wall in a corner of the car park, and now opening the boot she quickly dismantled the crossbow and stuffed all the component parts, the bolts and the empty strychnine vials into a black ruck sack.

Gemma locked the car, slung the rucksack over her shoulder and walked out of the hotel grounds towards the river Yonne which ran through the town. She walked south following the course of the river and after about twenty minutes she came to a wooded area that ran up to the edge of the river. Looking around her to make sure she was not being watched, she picked up a few large bits of rock and stone lying just off the path around her, put them in the ruck sack to weigh it down, and then checking once that nobody was watching, she slung the rucksack and its contents as far as she could into the centre of the river. It satisfyingly sank like the proverbial stone. Gemma returned to the hotel, had a shower, got changed into fresh clothes and at 5.00 am she paid her bill and drove out of Auxerre heading for Cannes.

'So what do we do now?' asked Colin. 'This wretched woman has beaten us to it yet again.'

'I have to admit' said Martin 'I quite admire her, not all the killings obviously, but the way she has gone about it. She set herself a mammoth task and has then gone about it in the most professional way possible. She left no clues as to what she was going to do next and so we have always been one step behind her. In all the murders she's committed she left no evidence anywhere that we could use in court, and what little we have got has only been obtained through an illegal break in. To be honest I'd love to sit chat with her, and in a funny way I'm a bit envious of Michael and Sam who've got to know her quite well.'

'I've come to the conclusion' I said 'that she believes there are two completely different people involved here.'

'What do you mean Michael?' asked Jo.

'Well Lady Louise is quiet, extremely courteous, and very generous and as far as we are aware, when she is in Lady Louise mode you couldn't wish to meet a nicer person.'

'Apart from the twenty one people she's murdered.' said Colin.

'No' I replied 'I think in her head that wasn't her. I honestly believe Lady Louise thinks she is completely innocent of all the killings and that they were done by Mrs Gemma Borgert who Lady Louise sees as someone else entirely.'

'You mean she's schizophrenic?' asked Sam.

'No, not in the true medical meaning of the word' I replied. 'I just think she gets herself into Mrs Borgert mode to do these killings and get her revenge, but the rest of the time she's a perfectly normal and happy go lucky woman.'

'Well that's both Martin and Michael' said George. 'Anyone else want to join the Lady Louise fan club?'

'Martin and Michael aren't saying that at all George' said Helena, 'and I must admit I do understand completely what they are saying. Can you imagine what pain and anguish you'd feel if the love of your life and your brand new wife of just twenty four hours had been killed by someone, you'd then had to watch her die in total agony in front of you, and not a soul did a dam thing to help? Then to cap it all the official authorities did absolutely nothing about it, just wrote it off and ended up not prosecuting anybody despite knowing exactly who had poisoned her. I think anyone under those circumstances might have gone a bit of the rails. I'm not approving of anything she's done, far from it, but I can understand it.'

'I see what you mean' said Colin 'but I still don't get this two different people thing. Lady Louise and Gemma Borgert are one and the same person, or am I the one going mad?'

'No you're right Colin' I said, 'physically they are as you say one and the same person, but I believe that in her head they are two totally different people, and I think she believes Lady Louise is not responsible for Gemma Borgert's actions.'

'Mmm' mused Colin 'I think I get what you're saying, but I still think we ought to arrest and prosecute Lady Louise.'

'Nobody is arguing with that' said Helena 'but before we can arrest and prosecute her, we have to find her, and we have no idea where she may have gone.'

'You can bet your life it's a long way from Paris' I said thinking aloud.

Gemma had in fact thought long and hard about it and she pretty soon decided not only did she need to get out of Paris, she needed to get out of France. The French police could hardly hunt her down if she wasn't in France, so checking what she needed to do and what route she would need to take on her laptop, she drove to the French town of Avignon. She left the hire car abandoned on the top floor of a really massive multi storey car park and then paid cash for a train ticket that would take her across the border to Madrid, the capital Spain. From Madrid she later caught another train, this time heading far to the South, and after a long and extremely tiresome bus journey she eventually arrived in the outskirts of Marbella where she took out a week long rental on a log cabin type holiday home adjacent to the beach. It wasn't luxurious, but she'd paid cash to the site Manager giving him a false name, and so it was totally anonymous. Nobody knew who she was or where she was. The cabin would be regularly cleaned by the team of maids, it had a fresh linen change every other day, it was all extremely well equipped including a full kitchen and with a large flat screen satellite TV in the lounge that received a large selection of British TV channels this particular accommodation would do her nicely while she worked out what the hell she was going to do with the rest of her life.

Chapter Thirty Two.

We were all sitting in Helena's hotel suite trying to decide what to do next.

'Well as I see it' began George 'she's totally screwed us. You can guarantee that if she's left the Four seasons then she knows we're on to her and that means in all probability she's not only left Paris, she's left France.'

'Oh I agree' said Helena. 'I also doubt she'll return to the UK, so the question is where has she gone and how do we find her?'

'Her credit card and bank transactions will show us where she's been won't they?' asked Sam.

'Yes' I agreed 'they will, but only if she uses them. Don't forget she's had several weeks to organize getting away, so I would imagine she's got a credit card in a false name we know nothing about. She's probably also got an off shore bank account she can pull money out of at any time in a name we know nothing about, but I'm pretty sure she'll just pay for everything in cash, therefore no paper trail.'

'So the question remains' said Colin 'What do we do now?'

'Well I see little point in any of us

remaining here is France, so I will go and see Detective Chief Inspector Claude Moreau and inform him that we sadly have no leads and have therefore decided to go back to Interpol's European headquarters in Amsterdam where we have much better facilities for tracing people. I won't tell him about Lady Louise as he'll only get annoyed with us for not keeping him fully informed, but I do think we did the right thing as we really didn't need the French police bulldozing their way through everything and screwing up any possible future prosecution.'

'So do you want Sam and me to come to Amsterdam as well?' I asked.

'Please guys, if you don't mind.' replied Helena. 'You know her better than any of us, and you may well think of something we don't. So can you all get packed please, and be ready to fly out on the Gulfstream in an hour. Oh and Martin, please be sure to bring the syringes of strychnine and Louise's diary with you.'

'Will do mien Führer' he replied sarcastically clicking his heels and saluting. Helena just looked at him as everyone else smiled.

Gemma was relaxing with a large glass of white wine, whilst lying on a sun lounger on the small private patio outside her log cabin which overlooked the Mediterranean. Her mind was in overdrive as to what to do and where to go. Her two personas were now dead to her. Obviously she couldn't go anywhere or do anything using the name Mrs Gemma Borgert as she'd be arrested immediately and sent to prison for the rest of her life. Fortunately the death penalty had been abolished in France back in February 2007, but Gemma thought life in prison would probably be worse. Legally she still has a passport and bank accounts in the name of Lady Louise Hamilton Smythe, but they were no use to her either as the minute she used them or tried to get back to the UK she would be arrested and suffer the same fate as Gemma would. So, what should she do?

Gemma had been thinking about it now for several days, in fact since she poisoned Raphael D'Aurevilly, the Executive Chef at Restaurant 'Seulement le meilleur'. She had opened an offshore bank account in the Cayman Islands several years ago, and over the previous three years she had transferred most of her wealth from her UK bank account to the Cayman Islands account simply because she knew her mother would find a way of poking her nose into her business if 'Lady Louise' had bought or did something she didn't approve of. Wanting total security and banking privacy she had done her research and the bank she had finally chosen in the Caymans did not require her name, just her money. After she had killed Raphael D'Aurevilly she moved the remainder of her money to the Cayman's leaving enough to settle her bill at the Four Seasons. Gemma now had access to several million US dollars, an open ended credit card and a debit card in the name of Miss Julia Mortimer. But the most important thing she now had was a completely legal passport in the same name.

Gemma had chosen the name of Julia Mortimer during her two weeks back in the UK immediately after Matthias had died. She realized that if she was going to poison numerous people and get her revenge on the people of Paris, then she was going to need a clean passport and an offshore bank account in a new name in order to make her escape and live a decent life after it was all over. She remembered reading a few years ago Frederick Forsyth's book 'The Day of the Jackal' in which he had described in great detail how to go about getting a genuine passport, but in a false name. She bought a copy of the paperback in W.H. Smith's and followed his instructions from the novel to the letter. Two days later she had been walking through her fourth church graveyard of the day in Newbury, searching for the right headstone when she saw the name Julia Mortimer on a very small white headstone. Examining the headstone she saw that Julia had sadly been killed in a road traffic accident aged just two and a half, just over thirty five years ago. That would have made her roughly thirty eight now and that would be fine for Gemma's needs. Gemma realized there was a ninety nine percent chance that neither the young Miss Julia Mortimer nor her parents had ever applied for a passport for the girl, so there was little chance of being found out. Gemma visited the local post office, got all the necessary passport application forms, a copy of the real Julia Mortimer's birth certificate which she obtained via a website that organizes copies of all sorts of legal documents, and then filling in all the various forms and including a couple of colour photographs of herself as Julia Mortimer, she took the whole lot to the passport office in London, where she paid the extra for a speedy response claiming she had been offered a last minute holiday with some friends due to leave in two weeks' time. Four hours very nervous hours of waiting later, Gemma received a perfectly legal passport in the name of Julia Mortimer that showed her details and her face. So whatever she did with the rest of her life Gemma would now be doing it as the extremely wealthy Miss Julia Mortimer.

The big question though was what on earth was she going to do, and where?

Gemma thought that after she had completed all the poisonings she would feel a sense of satisfaction that Matthias's death had been avenged, but so far she felt no satisfaction whatsoever, and she was beginning to think she never would. People tell you that time heals and you eventually get over the death of a loved one, or at least life becomes a little easier. But they were talking about losing your parents or a loved one through illness or old age, not seeing the love of your life die in complete agony in front of you. Gemma knew she would never be able to obliterate those images of Matthias rolling round the bed screaming in acute pain out of her brain, whatever she did and she now knew that in all probability, if her feelings didn't improve then she only really had one choice open to her.

Chapter Thirty Three.

We all flew into Amsterdam's Schiphol airport
and got a couple of cabs to take us to Helena's
Interpol HQ. Interpol's official European
headquarters is in Lyon in France, but when
Helena was asked to head up the European
Operations department, she specifically asked to
be based somewhere other than Lyon. She
wanted complete independence and to be able to
work without being watched twenty four hours
a day by other department heads. Interpol's
Commissioner Kurt Meisner, having held the
same position himself a few years earlier, fully
understood what Helena wanted and allowed
her to set up a headquarters for the Operations
department anywhere of her choosing.
Unsurprisingly, with Chief
Superintendent Helena Van Houten being
Dutch, she chose her home town of Amsterdam.

Interpol is a strange set up in many ways, and
most people think it has thousands of agents
wandering the world who can override the local
police and arrest anyone they choose whenever
they want. In fact nothing could be further from
the truth. Interpol is not a super international
police force that can arrest anyone it chooses,

and in fact Interpol has no agents or officers with the power to arrest anyone. Interpol functions primarily as a network of criminal law enforcement agencies from different countries, and it mostly offers administrative liaison among the law enforcement agencies of the member countries, providing communications and database assistance, mostly done through its central headquarters in Lyon. Unlike most national police databases, Interpol's databases can track criminals around the world by means of the authorized collection of fingerprints, facial photos, lists of wanted persons, DNA samples and travel documents.

Helena's department was very different however, as it is a purely investigative set up, with Helena having been given a massive amount of discretion in what her various department's agents can and can't do, but if during the course of their investigations they need to arrest anyone, then they must call on the local police force of whatever country they are operating in to do the arresting. Martin for example, having spent his formative years as South Africa's leading and most successful burglar still uses all those skills, but on behalf of Interpol, although that could never be admitted to the public, the press or even to the other departmental heads based in Lyon. Helena once described her department as being the modern equivalent of SOE, the Secret Operations Executive set up by Winston Churchill during the Second World War.

'So folks' she began with all of us sitting around the large conference table at the Amsterdam HQ building 'can I suggest we have a brain storming session. No idea is too stupid and we will consider any and all ideas as to how we go about finding Lady Louise Hamilton Smythe or Gemma Borgert, whichever you prefer.

'I very much doubt if she is using either name now' I suggested 'and if I was her I would have set up a fall-back position in a country other than France or the UK with separate finances available to me and a clean passport in another name.'

'Oh thanks a bunch Michael' said Jo smiling at me. 'Cheer us all up with your unbridled optimism for a speedy arrest and successful prosecution why don't you?'

'I know what you mean Jo' said Helena 'but I think Michael's right. We know she's not stupid, and most of what she's done has been carefully planned. I suspect she does have access to finances outside of those we know about, perhaps a Swiss or Luxemburg numbered bank account or maybe an offshore bank account somewhere, but I believe she will have set up something somewhere that will give her access to whatever cash she needs.'

'How about we start by checking the records of all her UK bank accounts?' suggested George. 'If she's transferred money out of them there may be records as to where it has gone, if you can persuade the receiving bank to tell you.'

'Despite the usual total anonymity assurances that most of these banks will give their customers' said Helena 'I have put pressure on them in the past and will have no hesitation in putting the same pressure on them in the future, particularly over this business with over twenty murders involved.'

'I'm not doubting you for a moment' said Sam 'but what sort of pressure can you put on an offshore or a Swiss bank. Surely Interpol has no authority?'

'Oh you're right, we don't officially' replied Helena 'but what we are most certainly allowed to do is investigate, that's part of our brief. A quiet word with the head of any one of these banks to the effect that if we don't get their full cooperation then we may be forced to inform the world's press, television and radio that Interpol will be thoroughly investigating that particular banks entire customer and client list in the very near future. It usually does the trick. They know full well that if that item of news were to be published, then that would result in the bank losing at least half of their richest clients overnight. But I always point out that if the bank chooses to cooperate fully with us, then Interpol will not say a word and leave them alone to carry on their business in peace and quiet.'

'Good grief Helena' said Sam 'you don't muck about do you? Thank God you're on my side. Remind me not to fall out with you.' Helena laughed.

'OK' she said 'So we look into her UK bank accounts. George, you've done this sort of investigation before, can I leave that one with you?'

'Sure' George replied 'but can I get Jo to help, she's also done this type of investigative work before.'

'Of course' replied Helena 'OK with you Jo?'

'Fine boss' she answered.

'OK' said Helena continuing. 'So next, where do we think she'll have gone? Ideas folks, preferably with reasons, not just a list of countries for the sake of it.'

'Well' I began 'we know Louise, and I'm going to stick with calling her Louise to avoid confusion, doesn't speak any foreign languages, well at least, not fluently. So my assumption is it would have to be somewhere where English is spoken or at least understood by most people.'

'OK, that makes sense' said Helena.

'I guess America is the obvious place' suggested Colin.

'Mmm' mused Martin 'in some ways it is, but to be honest I doubt it. It would need to be somewhere she can stay long term in necessary and she could probably get in to the States on a visitors passport, but I doubt if she could get a green card very easily and stay indefinitely. I think she'll stick to Europe with the EU's open borders policy where she can travel wherever she wants with no visa restrictions.'

'What about your own country of South Africa' asked Sam?

'A few year ago perhaps' replied Martin 'but not now. I don't even feel safe to walk around there on my own, never mind a good looking white woman. No, I think we can rule out South Africa. I think it has to be Europe.'

'I think that makes sense' I agreed 'and I

suppose the obvious choice would be the southern holidaymaker's resorts of Spain and Portugal. If it's somewhere the Brits go on holiday then the locals will all speak English. Forget Italy, Greece etc, they are great, but not enough of the locals speak English, and I think that will be essential for Louise to be able to survive.'

'Personally I think we can rule out Portugal' said Sam.

'Why?' I asked.

'Because before we thought of Louise as a friend and not as a murder suspect' answered Sam 'we told her that we both worked for Interpol. We told her we lived in the Algarve region of southern Portugal, where unlike most of the rest of Portugal everybody spoke English, and we also told her that the Algarve was quite a small community where everybody knew everybody else, particularly the Brits. I don't think she'd risk it.'

'That makes sense' said Helena. 'OK, let's start by concentrating on the southern coast of Spain then. Anywhere in particular spring to mind?'

'We know Louise doesn't like slumming it unless she has to' said Martin. 'I guess you could say she likes and demands the finer things in life, and I don't think she could change her attitudes that much, so to my mind that rules out places like Benidorm, Malaga, Fuengirola and Torremolinos. I think she'd set up shop somewhere where she could mix with her own type of rich people, and I guess the obvious places would be Majorca, Ibiza, the Canaries, Barcelona or Marbella.'

'I think you can rule out any islands' said Helena. 'I think Louise will want easy access for getting away in a hurry if necessary, and being trapped on an island with no way off other than a plane or a boat would rule it out for me.'

'OK, so that leaves us Barcelona or Marbella.' said Martin. 'Personally I'd plump for Marbella, it's more her sort of place.'

'OK then' said Helena. 'George, can you, Jo and Colin stay here where you have access to Interpol's database and start chasing down all Louise's financial affairs over the last six months. It could lead to something or it might take us nowhere. I'll leave the Gulfstream here at your disposal, hence the need for Colin to stay with you as co-pilots, and if you do need to visit an offshore bank and apply pressure personally, then just do it. Martin, you, Michael, Sam and me will get a flight to Marbella and see if we have any joy trying to find the elusive Louise.

It's a massive shot in the dark, but we have to start somewhere.'

Chapter Thirty Four.

George, Jo and Colin got started straight away in trying to trace Lady Louise's bank accounts. Within an hour they knew she had current accounts with both Barclays and Lloyds, a deposit account with Lloyds and an investment account with Coutts, a private bank and wealth management company. Originally founded in 1692, two years before the Bank of England was created, Coutts is the eighth oldest bank in the world, and has the added prestige of being 'the Queen's bank'. Having spoken at length to both Barclays and Lloyds, it was obvious that Louise only kept a relatively small amount of money with both, mainly for her day to day needs. The bank she kept most of her money with was Coutts, and it was to the manager of that esteemed organisation that George spoke.

'Graham' he began 'nice to speak with you again.'

Helena had asked George to investigate the financial side or Louise's affairs as he was the most experienced in these matters and had built a relationship with several top bank managers around the world. Graham Sullivan, the London manager of Coutts was one such manager who George had dealt with on numerous occasions.

'Don't tell me George' he replied 'you lot are after yet another one of my poor, innocent, law abiding customers?'

'Of course Graham' as you know Interpol exists purely and simply to annoy the world's leading bank managers. No, in all seriousness, I'm hoping you can help.'

'We'll do what we can as always' replied the bank manager.

'It may be important, but most likely it will lead nowhere. Are you familiar with a certain Lady Louise Hamilton Smythe, who I believe is one of your clients?'

'Was, not is' replied Graham. 'Strangely enough Lady Louise closed her account with us about six weeks or so ago, transferring every penny to a numbered account in Lichtenstein.'

'Was it a large account Graham' asked George.

'No, not really' replied the banker. 'Just over four million sterling, but we were happy to handle it for her as her father Lord Hamilton Smythe has banked with Coutts for over twenty five years now.'

'Can you give me all the details of the

Lichtenstein bank please Graham' requested George 'along with copies of Lady Louise's last six months statements. As I said earlier, it may be important, but most likely it will lead nowhere, but as lives are at stake we have no choice but to follow every possible lead.'

'No problem George, Coutts is always happy to help and cooperate with Interpol. I'll email everything to you straight away.'
And he did. Within six minutes of putting the phone down George had the details of the bank transfer to Lichtenstein. There were no names involved, just a series of numbers, the banks address, the manager's name and his telephone number. George handed Louise's Coutts bank statements to Colin and Jo and asked them to look for patterns, anything unusual, anything overseas etc, etc. George picked up the telephone again and dialled the private telephone number of the bank manager in Lichtenstein.

'Good morning Sir' George began 'May I speak please to Herr Maximilian Schneider. My name is Inspector George Copeland and I am a senior investigative officer with Interpol.'

'This is Maximilian Schneider speaking' he replied. 'May I ask how you got my personal telephone number?'

'Of course Herr Schneider, it was from a

fellow bank manager who is helping Interpol with our enquiries regarding a very serious matter in which we believe you too may be able to help.'

'I see' replied the bank manager. 'Most irregular, but I will help providing it doesn't conflict with the confidentiality of one of my clients.'

'Thank you' said George 'It relates to a private numbered account recently opened with yourselves in which you are holding over four million pounds sterling.'
George then gave Herr Schneider the seventeen digit account number.

'Usually' said the bank manager 'I would make no comment on such matters, but as we held the money you are referring to for less than an hour, I am happy to tell you we passed the money directly on to an offshore bank the lady had already selected and had an account with. Beyond that I can tell you nothing.'

'I see' said George thinking. 'Would it be possible to indicate to me somehow where this money ended up without breaking your confidentiality rules? This matter does involve the life and death of many people.'

'All I can say Mr Copeland is that if I were going on a sunshine holiday I wouldn't choose such a small flat island with far more businesses than people.'

'Thank you Herr Schneider, you have been most helpful.' and with that George replaced the telephone receiver on to its cradle. Colin and Jo had been listening in and Jo immediately asked:

'Did that last bit make any sense to you?'

'Oh perfectly' replied George. 'He is referring to the Cayman Islands in the Caribbean which as far as I remember has a total population of about 65,000 people, but there are over 100,000 businesses registered on the islands. It's also notoriously flat and incredibly boring if you don't like beaches and banks, which is about all the Cayman Islands has to offer visitors. There are roughly 160 banks on the main island and it is a complete waste of time trying to talk to any of them. They are on the world's black list and they won't divulge any information about anyone, which is of course their great attraction.'

'But surely that doesn't matter' said Colin. 'We now know Louise's money is all in a private Cayman Island bank account, and she has roughly four million sterling in that account. Even if we did know which specific bank, it wouldn't get us any further would it?'

'No' replied George 'I'll give Helena ring and let her know. They should all be in Marbella by now.'

Chapter Thirty Five.

Louise's thoughts were very far from the Cayman Islands. She was reviewing in her mind what she wanted to do with the rest of her life, and more realistically what she could do. She loved both her father and her mother, but there was no way she could risk going back to the UK to visit them. The danger of being arrested at an airport or at a ferry terminal were massive, and in all likelihood her parents were probably under constant surveillance just in case she turned up. If the UK police and Interpol were involved, which they obviously were then they were probably tapping her parents telephones in case she rang them. Apart from her parents, the only other person in her life that she had really loved was Matthias, and sadly that was all far too short. It was really strange and also completely unintentional, but the very second she thought about Matthias in her mind she became automatically stopped being Louise and became Mrs Gemma Borgert. It wasn't something she could control and she realised that this was how it was going to be for the rest of her life. However, Gemma also knew that due to her careful planning and the near perfect execution of her revenge plan, she now had the chance to live a full and active life as Julia Mortimer anywhere in the world she chose, with more money than she knew what to do with. No, she corrected herself, these days four million was not the fortune it once was, and despite having poisoned twenty one people and completed her revenge plan in full, she was sad and disappointed that she felt no satisfaction and no sense of peace whatsoever. Perhaps the satisfaction and peace would come with time. She hoped so. She then closed her eyes, stretched out on the sun lounger and decided to soak up the afternoon sun in Marbella before going out for a meal.

Helena, Sam, Martin and myself arrived in Marbella and based ourselves in Marriott's Beach Resort. Helena had organised it, and booked us all in as guests of a member who owned timeshare with Marriott's. It was very comfortable and we were allocated a three bedroom apartment. Sam and I had been kindly given the master, with Helena taking the second bedroom and Martin getting the third, although in all honesty they were all more or less the same. There was also a large lounge, a full kitchen and a large balcony with sea views.

'Well I've stayed in worst places' I said smiling.

'Yes, well don't get too comfortable' said Helena 'we're here to work, not to sunbathe and swim. Well, not much anyway' she laughed.

'So what's the plan?' asked Martin.

'To be honest' replied Helena 'nothing very complicated. All we can really do is search for her among the masses of various holiday accommodations stretched out along the beach front. I suggest Michael and Sam go right and Martin and I go left. We just walk along the beach front and see if we can spot her.'

'She may not be in Marbella' said Sam.

'She may not even be in Spain' said Martin 'or come to that she may not be in Europe anymore, but I guess we have to start somewhere, and when we went through the various possibilities, this seemed the most logical place to start.'

'Come on' said Helena. 'Let's get looking, and we'll meet back here in the resorts beach bar at 5.00 pm for a drink and a snack. Good luck.' We all left, and as Helena had suggested Sam and I went to the right while Helena and Martin went off to the left. None of us were very hopeful.

Gemma had been dozing in and out of sleep for just over an hour and a half, and she now needed a cool drink. She got up from the sun lounger, walked inside the log cabin and poured herself a glass of chilled white wine from the bottle she'd put in the fridge earlier in the day. She was standing in the shade just inside the patio doors taking advantage of and enjoying the cool of the cabin's air conditioning, casually watching the numerous holidaymakers outside. Some were just passing by, others were swimming in the sea, several people were chatting with each other on their sun loungers while their kids played with a ball in the water, when Gemma suddenly noticed a woman she thought she vaguely recognized walking along the beach. The woman had a full head of long blonde hair, and Gemma thought for a moment it was Sam, but then she dismissed it from her mind, that would be crazy and far too much of a coincidence. Then suddenly the woman stopped, turned around towards her now facing the cabin, but Gemma then realized the woman wasn't looking at the log cabin, she was saying something to the man walking about four feet behind her. There was now no doubt, the man she was talking to she was one hundred percent sure was Michael, and now she could see her full face there was no doubt, the woman was most definitely Sam. Gemma automatically ducked down in the lounge area and assumed they'd traced her here and found the log cabin, God knows how but obviously they had. She panicked slightly, but then as she watched them from the shadows inside the cabin, she calmed down as she realized they actually had no idea she was there or that she'd seen them. A sense of quiet calm came over her again, however, she realized that they were not here by accident and it was a pretty sure bet they weren't on here their own. Somehow they'd worked out she was here, and of one thing Gemma was now very sure. She could not stay here in Marbella a moment longer than she had to.

Gemma waited for Michael and Sam to disappear from sight, and once they had gone she quickly packed everything she had with her and threw it all into the back of the hire car, a silver BMW 5 series. Gemma left the resort and drove west along the coast road as far as Estepona and then took the winding road inland up through the hills towards Seville. The drive was beautiful, but Gemma never noticed the landscape at all. It took a couple of hours during which she had time to think long and hard about the future that lay before her. By the time she reached Seville Gemma had made her decision, and she knew she would not be changing her mind.

Chapter Thirty Six

Sam and I had returned to the Marriott's resort as had Helena and Martin. The four of us sat in comfortable armchairs having a beer in the beach bar.

'Well we've spent two full days searching all the resorts along the coast' said Martin 'and to be honest I'm not sure what else we can do. If she is here she's certainly well hidden.'

'Don't forget coming here was a total shot in the dark' said Helena 'but failing all else it was worth a try.'

'Tell me again' said Sam. 'What was it exactly that George said about Louise's bank accounts?'

'There's not too much to tell' replied Helena. George said she had UK bank accounts with Barclays, Lloyds and Coutts, and it was Coutts that had the bulk of her money, just over four million US dollars, but then about six or seven weeks ago she moved the whole lot to an offshore bank on the Cayman Islands. We don't know which one, but to be perfectly frank it wouldn't make any difference if we did know. I'm afraid the Cayman Island banks are the most uncooperative in the world, and they are all a law unto themselves, refusing to tell any of the world's various law enforcement agencies anything about any of their clients.'

'Why six weeks ago?' asked Sam. 'Did something happen that triggered it or was she always planning to move the money and had only just got round to it.'

'I suspect' I said 'that she was waiting to see how her plan worked out and was waiting to make sure it was going to plan before making her move.'

My phone rang and apologising to the others for the interruption, I answered it.

'Good morning Michael' said a voice I recognised. It was Louise.

'Good morning to you too Louise' I said and turned on the speaker for the benefit of the others who had all stopped talking and were suddenly all ears.

'Do you really like Marbella or were you just missing me?' she asked.

'So you are in Marbella' I asked?

'Was Michael, was. The minute I saw you and Sam walking along the beach I packed up and left. Oh and by the way' she said 'I have bought myself a new burner mobile phone, so don't bother trying to trace me through my old mobile which as you have probably realised by now I haven't turned on for quite a while. But what I am interested to know is how you knew I'd gone to Marbella?'

'We didn't' I answered honestly 'we just tried to put ourselves in your shoes and go where we thought you would go. I guess we were right, but sadly you saw us before we saw you.'

'Yes, well Spain would have done me nicely for a while, but thanks to you and Sam that's not a possibility any more is it, and yes, to save you asking, I'm not in Spain anymore and no, I'm not going to tell you where I am now.'

'I would love to sit down with you sometime' I said 'and really try to get to grips with what you've done and try to understand why you felt it was necessary to murder twenty one people, most of whom were totally innocent.'

'I tell you what Michael, I'll meet you and Sam underneath the Eifel Tower at 10.00 am two weeks from today, and I'll tell you everything. If you bring any of the others or inform the French police I will know and you'll never hear from me again.'

'So have I got this right' I asked. 'You'll meet Sam and me underneath the Eifel Tower at 10.00 am on Wednesday the 21st?'

'Correct' replied Louise 'but just you two. Nobody else, and don't forget, I'll know if you two aren't alone. Bye Michael, I'll see you in two weeks.'

The phone connection was suddenly cut off and we just sat and stared at each other.

'Well what do you make of that' I asked?

'I'm surprised she wants to meet up, but it proves your thinking was right Michael' said Helena 'she had gone to Marbella and if she hadn't have been lucky enough to see you and Sam we may well have caught her.'

'But do we go to the Eifel Tower in two weeks' time?' Sam asked.

'Most definitely' answered Helena. 'And to save you asking we'll be near, but well out of sight and not visible. We'll wire you up so that we can hear and record everything, and if necessary we'll come and grab her.'

'But why offer to meet us?' queried Sam again. 'She must realize she stands every chance of being arrested.'

'But not by you two' said Helena. 'Don't forget, as Interpol officers we have no powers of arrest, but leaving that aside I think there's something else going on here. I can't put my finger on it, but she's got something in mind, and I guess we've got two weeks to try and work out what.'

There was nothing else to do in Spain, so the four of us caught the first flight we could returning to Amsterdam's Schiphol airport, and from the airport we went straight to Helena's HQ building. The next day we sat around Helena's office not really knowing what we could do, if anything, and then Sam had a great idea.

'Why don't Michael and I fly to the UK and make an unannounced visit to Louise's parents. We can just call in as friends who happened to be in the area. We don't mention anything that's happened in France or that we work for Interpol. Michael is simply a crime thriller writer and I'm just a doctor. All perfectly true. You never know, they may accidentally let something drop if Louise has been in touch with them, but I don't see that there's anything to lose.'

'Great idea Sam. George, can you, Colin and Jo take the Gulfstream and fly Sam and Michael to the UK first thing tomorrow. I'm not sure where the nearest airport will be, but whichever it is it'll be a lot nearer and quicker than taking a commercial flight.'

'Southampton will be the closest commercial airport' said Colin. 'I think it's roughly thirty miles away from Newbury.'

'OK, take them there then' said Helena 'and then bring them both back after the meeting. If you all end up having to stay overnight then do so.'

'Is there anything the rest of us, ie you and me can do boss?' asked Martin.

'I wish there was, but with no evidence to examine, no leads to follow up, no witnesses to interview and no idea where on the planet she is, we are to use that lovely English expression - stuffed!'

'I hate to say this again' said Martin 'but in so many ways I really admire her. If I was still having criminal thoughts, which of course I'm not as I'm now a model citizen and the pride of Interpol, but if I was, I'd recruit her to my team tomorrow.'

'Careful Martin' said Sam laughing 'you'll be proposing to her next.'

'Well be fair to her Sam' Martin said 'she is also really good looking as well as having a great brain.'

'I do believe the poor besotted man is in love' I said laughing.

'You can laugh' said Martin 'but leaving aside the fact she's murdered twenty one people in cold blood and is France's most notorious serial killer since the Second World War, she has a lot of excellent redeeming features.'
Martin laughed as Sam through a cushion at him.

The next day George flew us to Southampton in the Gulfstream, with Colin in the co-pilot's seat and Jo playing the hostess with the mostest, her favourite role. We picked up a hire car at the airport and Sam and I drove to the home of Lord and Lady Hamilton Smythe. The house was built of Cotswold coloured stone and was every inch a Palladian mansion in both its style and size. Set in over seventy acres of manicured gardens, lawns and trees, it had privacy and a long gravel drive was lined with hundreds of tall Cyprus trees. We pulled up outside and a man in his late sixties or early seventies came out of the front door and walked down the steps to greet us.

'Good morning' he said greeting us

cheerfully 'I'm Charlie Smith, but don't let my wife know I still use my old name at times, she prefers I use Lord Charles Hamilton Smythe.' He laughed.

'Good morning Your Lordship' I replied. 'I'm Michael Turner and this is my wife Samantha.' We all shook hands and as we did so I continued 'We met your daughter Louise in Paris several weeks ago and we ended up becoming really good friends, but then she left Paris and I'm afraid we lost track of her. She'd mentioned the wonderful home you have here and as we were in the area we thought we would call by on the off chance she was here.'

'No, I'm afraid she's not' replied his Lordship 'To be honest Michael we haven't seen her for a couple of months now, although she does telephone either myself or the good lady wife occasionally and let us know what she's up to.'

I bet she hasn't told you what she's been up to in Paris I thought, but I said nothing.

'So you've no idea where she is now then your Lordship?' asked Sam

'Not a clue my dear, and its Charlie, not your Lordship, alright?' he said

'Fine by us Charlie' I replied.

'Anyway, where are my manners' Charlie

said. 'Come into the house, meet the wife and have a cup of tea.'

We entered the house and were staggered at the size and opulence of the interior. Charlie led us through the marbled hall with rich maroon and gold carpets and into a massive drawing room. Lady Hamilton Smythe was sitting in a large upholstered chair reading a fashion magazine. She looked up as we entered and put down the magazine as she rose out of the chair.

'A couple of visitors for us my dear' said Charlie. 'Michael and Samantha, good friends of Louise's who all met in Paris and they decided to pay their respects as they were passing. Oh and by the way, I've told them to call me Charlie, so none of this 'me Lord' nonsense you love so much.'

'Good morning to you both' his wife said totally ignoring her husband and addressing us. 'I'm Lady Emily Hamilton Smythe, and I'm pleased to meet you both. Unlike my husband I however prefer to stick to the correct forms of address.'

'Good morning your ladyship' I replied 'Louise has spoken of you quite a lot, and you too Charlie of course.'

'And what may I ask do you two folk do? asked Lady Emily. 'Are you both in some form of trade?'

'I am a writer and novelist' I replied 'and Sam here is a doctor.'

'Oh, so you work for the National Health Service then' said Lady Emily, as if it was an accusation and the NHS was beneath her.

'Oh good grief no' replied Sam playing the game. 'I own and run an extremely successful private medical practice in the Algarve region of southern Portugal. In fact we are located in the middle of Quinta do Lago, one of the most expensive patches of real estate in the whole of southern Europe.'

'Oh excellent' smiled Lady Emily cheering up no end. Words like what a pompous bloody snob sprang to mind, but I behaved myself and held my tongue.

Sam had smiled at Charlie as she'd spoken, and realizing what Sam had done he immediately smiled back with a 'I know what you're really thinking' look on his face. You could tell that he agreed, but he loved his wife so he said nothing. At this point the butler entered, well I assumed he was the butler.

'Ah James' said Lady Emily 'Tea for four please.'

James nodded, said nothing and departed.

'So Michael' said Lady Emily 'you said

earlier that you are a writer. What sort of books do you write?'

'Oh I don't know as you'd approve of my books my lady' I replied 'I'm afraid I write crime thrillers.'

'Excellent' she beamed 'I love crime thrillers.'

'We have bookcases full of them upstairs' said Charlie laughing.

'Have you had any of them published' she asked?

'Yes' I replied smiling 'All of them.'
Lady Emily suddenly went deep into thought, and then she said,

'You're not Michael Turner by any chance are you?'

'Well as it happens I am' I replied. 'You've heard of me?'

'Heard of you' she gushed 'I've read every word you've published and Lord Charles and I are now planning a trip around Europe based around your excellent crime based travel guides. I'm dying to see where all those ghastly murders took place. Oh how wonderful, Michael Turner in my house. Charles, if Michael doesn't mind could you take a photograph of us together?'

'Not at all' I said smiling. Perhaps Lady

Emily wasn't so bad after all. At least she had excellent taste in authors. Charlie took a couple of photographs and then James reappeared with a pot of tea and four cups and saucers.

'So you two' said Lady Emily 'tell me what my wayward daughter has been up to. Michael come and sit next to me, Sam please make yourself comfortable. So how did you meet Louise?'

We recounted the stories of meeting Louise, going to the theatre with her, visiting art galleries, the ballet etc although we obviously said nothing about the poisonings.

'You say she's left Paris' asked Charlie? 'Any idea where she is now, only we haven't heard from her for weeks and her mobile phone seems to be turned off.'

'No idea I'm afraid Charlie' I replied. 'We were hoping she might be here or at least you'd know where we could catch up with her.'

'Nope, haven't a clue I'm afraid.' He said

'Please don't say nope dear' commanded Lady Emily 'it sounds so awfully working class.'

'In case you've forgotten my Lady' said Charlie as sarcastically as he could muster and putting on a cockney accent 'I am flippin' workin' class, and despite all yer fancy posh word, yer airs an' graces and lar-di-dar mannerisms, you were also workin' class when we first met.'

'Yes I am fully aware of that dear' replied Lady Emily 'but some of us have chosen to move on in life as I'm sure Michael and Samantha here appreciate.'

'Whatever you say dear' he retorted smiling at his wife and both of us.
We carried on chatting pleasantly for another fifteen minutes or so, but it was obvious they had no idea where their daughter was or what she'd been doing in Paris, so we said our thank you's and our goodbye's and left.

Chapter Thirty Seven.

We flew back to Amsterdam, this time with Colin at the controls, and having left the Gulfstream in its usual hanger we drove to Helena's HQ in the city centre. The next few days were to be honest pretty boring as far as the case was concerned. Unlike the French police, we knew exactly who the Paris poisoner was, but if we were going to stand any chance of apprehending her then the last thing we needed was the Paris police trampling all over the case and scaring Louise off from our rendezvous. There was nothing we could so as we had no idea where Louise was or what name she was using, all we had was a time and place to meet. So we waited.

Wednesday the 21st duly arrived and all of us were back in Paris having flown in on the Gulfstream the previous day. Helena, Martin, George, Colin and Jo were all wearing listening devices the size of hearing aids, and what they were listening to was the input from the wires Sam and myself were both wearing. In the old days a wire was literally that, a length of cable with a microphone at one end, but these days with the arrival of Bluetooth and the ever decreasing size of electronic components, a wire can be really small and be made to look like a badge, a brooch, a button, anything you can think of. At 9.45 am Sam and I wandered over to the foot of the Eifel Tower and stood underneath the structure waiting for 10.00 am to arrive.
At 9.55 am my mobile rang and it was Louise on the other end.

'Good morning Michael, nice and punctual I see.'

'Well I was brought up to never keep a lady waiting, my lady.' I replied.

'Mmm, very droll Michael. I cannot see any of your colleagues, but I assume they are within running distance of the Eifel Tower and that you and Sam are both wired. Please don't bother denying it, because I wouldn't believe you anyway.'

'Oh I wouldn't dream of denying it, yes we are both wired for sound and yes our Interpol colleagues are all within easy running distance but they will keep their distance as long as our lives are not threatened by you.'

'Of course they are not Michael. I think of you and Sam as my friends, despite what I have done over the last few weeks, so you are both perfectly safe as far as I'm concerned.'

'Listen Louise, lovely as it is having this phone call with you, we could easily have done this while we were still in Amsterdam. Are you planning on meeting as we agreed?'

'Of course Michael. Why don't you and Sam come up and join me. I am on the top platform of the tower, and I have to say the views from here are magnificent.'
The line went dead, and Sam and I just looked at each other.

'Well I suppose we get the lift then?' asked Sam?

'Well I'm buggered if I'm going to walk up all the damn stairs. There are 1,665 of them, although the section between the second platform and the top is closed to the public, I presume to stop people jumping off.'

'You don't think that's what Louise has in mind do you' Sam asked?

'God, I've no idea what goes on in that woman's mind.' I said 'The death of her husband obviously affected her in so many ways and turned the friendly, funny, gentle soul we know as Lady Louise Hamilton Smythe into the mass murderer we know as Gemma Borgert, so to be honest, I've no idea what she wants.'

'So, the lift it is then.' said Sam, and we joined the lengthy queue to get the various lifts that would get us to the top. I suppose this is as good a time as any to mention the fact that I suffer from vertigo, and to honest standing on a chair can make me feel giddy. So I was not looking forward to 'the wonderful views from the top' that other people might. The queue for tickets wasn't too bad and we were in the first lift within 5 minutes. That lift took us to the second level in about three minutes, and then we caught the second lift which took about five minutes to get us to the top. Stepping out of the lift and onto the large platform I realised I would be alright. Although my vertigo is pretty bad, it is not a problem if I have something solid under my feet and I am enclosed with no easy way of falling off. Needless to say, unlike my wife's dare devil attitude to heights, the edge of tall cliffs are not my favourite picnic locations, but that's another story.

We emerged from the lift and walked in a clockwise direction from left to right, and turning a corner we saw Louise standing with her back to the fencing which surrounded the top platform ensuring nobody fell off. We approached her and stopped about two to three feet away.

'Good morning both of you' she said smiling. 'Thank you for coming all the way up here to meet me. Oh, and by the way, let me start by saying I have no intention of being arrested by you or any of your colleagues. I have no wish to use it as I think of you two as my friends, but if you try to grab me, I will not hesitate in the slightest about shooting you both.'
Louise pulled back one side of her jacket with her left hand showing that her right hand was holding a handgun of some sort. I couldn't be sure, but to me it looked like a Glock, although whatever it was I had no intention of finding out.

'We have no intention of grabbing you' I said 'and even if we wanted to, we couldn't arrest you because Interpol has no powers of arrest. It always down to the local police, and we haven't even mentioned your name to the French police. We just want to talk to you and find out why a truly lovely woman has turned into a serial killer?'

'We flew to England last week and had tea with your parents' said Sam. 'We never mentioned any of the poisonings etc and just said we'd met you in Paris and became good friends. Your dad is great, he's really down to earth and we discovered your mum absolutely loves Michael's books and has read them all. She even made your father take a photograph of your mum and Michael together.'

'Yes' I said. 'She even made me sign all my books before we left.'

'Well thank you for not telling them about the poisonings' said Louise 'it would greatly upset them both, and unlike me they've done nothing wrong and shouldn't be made to suffer by people staring at them and pointing fingers.'

'Tell me Louise' said Sam in a very gentle voice 'why all the killings. Why couldn't you have simply gone to the police, complained about everything that had happened and then let the law take its course?'

'Because nothing would have happened'

she replied vehemently. 'The police told me in no uncertain terms that Matthias's death was just an accidental poisoning and that neither the chef nor the owner would face any sort of prosecution.'

'OK' said Sam, 'but leaving that aside, why murder seven innocent people in the restaurant that first night we were in Paris. Thank God neither Michael nor I had tomatoes with our meal or we'd be dead as well.'

'And I would have very much regretted that, but at the time I was not only furious with the chef, the owner of the restaurant and the doctor who let Matthias die, I was just as angry at the attitude of the French, both the police and the general attitude of the people. Despite saving their butts in the Second World War and giving them their country back, they all have this bloody superior attitude that they are somehow better than everybody else. Their food and cuisine is supposedly better than anyone else's, that's total crap, and it's not. According to the French their wine is supposedly the best in the world, again total rubbish, Australian wines are much better as are several others from around the world, but the French just can't accept it. It's the same with everything, and it's even worse in Paris than in the rest of France. No, the French needed to understand they are not the greatest nation in the world, as far as I'm concerned no nation is superior to any other, and that first night was my way of teaching the damn French a lesson they wouldn't forget in a hurry.'

'Tell me' I asked. 'Why did you poison all those doctors? It could have been far more because of the random way you went about it, but why? They'd done you no harm, they just spent their lives trying to heal people.'

'You have to try and understand the state of mind I was in. Matthias was the first man I had ever really loved. Yes I'd had boyfriends before, but nothing like the love I felt for my husband. It was all consuming and I had that love taken away from me within days of being married. If the medical profession of Paris had done their job properly then a doctor could have been with Matthias within minutes and no doubt saved his life. But nobody bothered did they?'

'But that was one particular doctor who failed you' said Sam 'not all doctors.'

'No, it was the attitude of the whole medical profession. When I telephoned I told them it was very serious food poisoning and my husband was dying as we spoke. They could have sent an ambulance straight away, but they didn't. They could have checked how long the doctor they did call would be, but they didn't. They could have got a paramedic to race to the scene, but they didn't. They made one phone call to a doctor who was already tied up with another patient and then did nothing. That was the fault of the French medical system. Yes, looking back, my actions at the time were extreme and I now regret the random killings, but I do not regret killing the doctor, the chef and the restaurant owner.'

'So what now Louise' asked Sam?

'I know it is over for me Sam. I'm not stupid and that's why I chose to meet you here. I actually came to this exact spot yesterday and spent quite a bit of time when nobody was looking using some very strong bolt cutters hidden inside a thick overcoat to cut through a section of the wire I'm standing in front of. I bent it back so that it would not be noticed, but I opened the gap this morning while I was standing here in front of it waiting for you'

I realised what she was saying and in all probability was about to do and took a step forward. She opened the jacket again and pointed the gun at me.

'Please don't make me kill you two as well Michael. Let me do this, it's better for everyone. Just promise me my parents will never know what I've done. When I lost my dear husband Matthias so soon after being married, I became two different people. I was still the fun loving and carefree Louise I'd always been, but sadly I also became the vengeful Gemma Borgert, and I now realize I handled everything so badly. I thought that avenging the death of my dear Matthias would bring me a real sense of lasting peace. But I now realize nothing ever will, and if anything I now feel even worse. I know there is no future for me now, and even though I could run from the authorities, I would eventually get caught and I couldn't cope with spending the rest of my life in prison, but even worse, the pain I feel at his loss gets worse and worse every day and I can't stand it anymore, so I go to be with my Matthias. Goodbye my friends.'

Now holding the gun out in front of her to prevent anyone from interfering, Louise stepped to one side and quickly squeezed through the narrow gap in the wire she had created. Once through she pushed the wire back in place and closed the gap as people seeing what was happening now started screaming. Louise looked at both Sam and I, and then blowing us both a kiss and stepped backwards. We both rushed to the fence and looked down, it was a sight I'll never forget. Because the Eifel Tower gets wider and wider as it gets nearer its base, Louise had crashed into a section of the ironwork and that pushed her even further out. She kept falling and once again she crashed into more of the structural ironwork. We never saw her hit the ground, but from the sound coming from below it seemed like half of Paris was screaming.

Chapter Thirty Eight
Epilogue.

There was no way Louise's death could be hidden from the public or the press, but nobody apart from the seven of us knew the real reason. We sat in our hotel room and discussed it all at length. Martin's argument eventually won the day, which was basically why tell anyone that Louise was actually Mrs Gemma Borgert, the Paris Poisoner. It wouldn't bring anyone back, she couldn't be punished because she was already dead. The Paris Police would never forgive Interpol in a thousand years for keeping them in the dark over who Louise really was and Louise's poor parents, now in their later years would never be able to show their faces in public again. So we kept what we knew to ourselves.

Louise's body was eventually released for burial or cremation, and Sam and I, with Helena's agreement took it upon ourselves to take the body back to her parents. We flew over in the Gulfstream with the whole team, and having cleared and sorted all the paperwork, we drove to the house of her parent's followed by the black van carrying Louise's coffin. We had telephoned two days earlier and had told Charlie that we would ensure Louise's body was returned to them. I had in fact telephoned Charlie less than an hour after Louise had thrown herself backwards of the Eifel Tower, as the last thing I wanted them to do was discover the news via the TV or radio. Needless to say, both Charlie and Lady Emily were distraught, not only over their daughter's death but also the manner of her death. There was no way of hiding the truth about what had happened, but at least we could hide the real reason. Sam, being a doctor, told them Louise had for months been suffering from bouts of severe depression which she'd been hiding from everyone, which was basically true, and despite the various medications she was on, she had decided she could take no more. Unfortunately, a Swedish tourist who was also on the top platform of the tower had filmed everything from the first scream when Louise pointed the gun at us, and then stepped back through the gap in the wire fence. He then gave the film to the main French TV network who broadcast it in France that night and then they sold the rights to anyone else willing to pay for them. Charlie and Lady Emily had seen the Swedish clips on the Channel Four news in the UK.

Sam and I stayed on for the funeral, which all seven of us attended. It meant a lot to Charlie and his wife and Louise was quietly buried in a very private quiet spot in the garden at the rear of the house. We left their house and needing to switch off, George flew us all to the Algarve. Everyone stayed with us for a couple of days and then Helena, Martin, George, Colin and Jo bade us farewell and flew on to Amsterdam. As for Sam and I, well our holiday in Paris was no holiday whatsoever, so we trawled the internet looking for something relaxing where nothing could go wrong. To that end we found ourselves an excellent week long cruise leaving Seattle in a month's time and visiting Alaska. I'd always wanted to visit the Klondike.

THE END

Printed in Poland
by Amazon Fulfillment
Poland Sp. z o.o., Wrocław